READ ME
MORE STORIES

Compiled by the Child Study Association
of America, inc.

Illustrated by Barbara Cooney

NEW YORK: THOMAS Y. CROWELL COMPANY

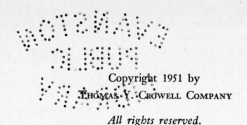
Acknowledgments

For the privilege of reprinting the following copyrighted poems and stories, grateful acknowledgment and thanks are extended to the sources indicated:

Dorothy Aldis, "Little" from *Everything and Anything*, copyright 1925, 1926, 1927 by Dorothy Aldis, courtesy of G. P. Putnam's Sons.

Laura Bannon, *Red Mittens*, reprinted by permission of and arrangement with Houghton Mifflin Company, the authorized publishers.

Edna Becker, *900 Buckets of Paint*, copyright 1949 by Pierce and Smith, reprinted by permission of Abingdon-Cokesbury Press, publishers.

Margaret Wise Brown, *The Runaway Bunny*, copyright 1942 by Harper & Brothers, reprinted by permission of the publisher.

Dorothy and Marguerite Bryan, *Tammie and That Puppy*, copyright 1936 by Dorothy M. Bryan, reprinted by permission of Dodd, Mead & Company, publisher.

Madye Lee Chastain, *The Sailboat*, reprinted by permission of Whitman Publishing Company, publisher.

Ruth Cording, "Luke and his Little Red Wagon" reprinted by permission of *Children's Activities*, the original publisher.

Margaret Farquhar, "Mr. Zooly's Zoo," reprinted by permission of *Child Life*.

Virginia Howell, *Who Likes the Dark?* reprinted by permission of Lothrop, Lee & Shepard Co., Inc., publisher.

Jessie Orton Jones, "Houses" (Poem XXI) from *Secrets*, illustrated by Elizabeth Orton Jones, copyright 1945 by Jessie Orton Jones and Eliza-

Preface

"The children love these stories—we have worn both volumes thin! Haven't you some more stories for us?"

This plea from a father of two young children started us on another quest. We weren't sure: would we be able to find and bring together still another collection of just-right stories for that insatiable read-to-me age?

Here is the third collection! Here, again, within one cover, is a story feast for young listeners. It has all the things the littlest ones love to hear about: children and families, creatures and outdoor things, circuses and pets and balloons, trucks and boats and trains. There are familiar sights and sounds as well as the oddest happenings, everyday doings as well as the most utter nonsense. Everything under the sun is here, served up for the wonder and delight of small children.

The Children's Book Committee of the Child Study Association of America has made this book for parents, teachers, and librarians—for all, in fact, who have children in their charge—with the hope that it will provide a shared pleasure, a very special bond of mutual enjoyment between them and their young listeners. All the members of the committee are parents; some are also teachers, librarians, children's story writers. Their selections have been based on their knowledge of children's interests and their experience with family tastes and group needs, at home, in nursery school, and wherever there are children.

In selecting these stories and verses for the youngest, the committee was mindful, too, of older brothers and sisters who are just beginning to read. These children need just a bit of a story, not too hard to be inviting but not too easy to be interesting, with pictures scattered throughout to break up the pages and let the reader pause.

Some of the stories and verses in this book were written especially for this collection. Others have appeared in various forms elsewhere, some in magazines, some as separate books. All of them are modern.

Barbara Cooney has again drawn upon her intimate knowledge of children to fill the pages of our collection with her joyous pictures, at once winsome and humorous, with those endearing details young children love to pore over.

As before, the book represents the creative collaboration of many people. To the artist and writers who have given it the breath of life—many of them already high favorites with young readers—the committee is deeply grateful for the privilege of presenting them in this book. To Elizabeth Riley, Editor of Children's Books of the Thomas Y. Crowell Company, goes our special appreciation for her wise unraveling of knotty problems and her unfailing readiness to surmount the hurdles. To the members of the committee who have worked tirelessly and anonymously, and especially to its chairman, Mrs. Hugh Grant Straus, whose vision and enthusiasm turn each challenge to a triumph, belongs most of the credit for this as for our earlier *Read-to-Me* storybooks.

Above others, one member of the committee, Bella Koral, has given to this book the imprint of her special genius for selection and collection. Her sensitivity and skilled research have furnished the magnet which pulled each story and verse into its particular niche.

We hope the children and their parents will enjoy reading this book as much as we have enjoyed making it.

JOSETTE FRANK
Staff Advisor
Children's Book Committee

Contents

WAKE UP, FARM!

by ALVIN TRESSELT

All through the night while everything was asleep, the bright stars shone in the sky.

Now it was time for the sun to come up, and the sky grew light. First one, then two, then all the birds began to sing their morning songs.

Wake up, Farm!

The big fat barnyard rooster heard them and he hopped down from his high perch. "Cock-a-doodle-doo," he crowed. Wake up, Farm!

1

"Cluck, cluck, cluck," the chickens woke up, jumped down on the ground and started to eat corn.

The horse woke up in her stall and licked her baby colt behind the ears.

The white ducks came out of the bushes, wiggled their tails and jumped into the brook for a swim.

"Quack, quack, quack." Wake up, Farm!

"Grunt grunt," the pigs woke up and waddled about their pen looking for breakfast.

The gray goose woke up in the grass with her baby goslings around her.

"Honk, honk, honk." Wake up, Farm!

The donkey woke up and wiggled his long soft ears. He looked very sleepy.

The turkey woke up in the apple tree. He ruffled his feathers and called, "Gobble, gobble, gobble."

The sheep woke up and came out of the barn to eat the shiny wet grass.

The sleepy pigeons flew out of their nest and circled over the barn. "Coo, coo, coo."

The tabby cat woke up and purred as she gave her kittens their morning bath.

The dog woke up in his kennel and barked at a noisy chipmunk.

"Bow, wow wow!" Wake up, Farm!

The rabbit woke up, twitched his nose, and ate a carrot for his breakfast.

The bees came out of their hives and buzzed around in the pink clover.

"Buzz, buzz, buzz." Wake up, Farm!

The cows woke up and stood by the pasture gate, waiting to be milked.

And at last the farmer came out with his shiny milk pails, just as the sun rose up over the hill.

A little boy in the big farmhouse woke up and stretched.

There was the sun shining in his window.

Good Morning!

THE RUNAWAY BUNNY

by MARGARET WISE BROWN

Once there was a little bunny who wanted to run away.

So he said to his mother, "I am running away."

"If you run away," said his mother, "I will run after you. For you are my little bunny."

"If you run after me," said the little bunny, "I will become a fish in a trout stream and I will swim away from you."

"If you become a fish in a trout stream," said his mother, "I will become a fisherman and I will fish for you."

"If you become a fisherman," said the little bunny, "I will become a rock on the mountain, high above you."

"If you become a rock on the mountain high above me," said his mother, "I will be a mountain climber, and I will climb to where you are."

"If you become a mountain climber," said the little bunny, "I will be a crocus in a hidden garden."

"If you become a crocus in a hidden garden," said his mother, "I will be a gardener. And I will find you."

"If you are a gardener and find me," said the little bunny, "I will be a bird and fly away from you."

"If you become a bird and fly away from me," said his mother, "I will be the tree that you come home to."

"If you become a tree," said the little bunny, "I will become a little sailboat, and I will sail away from you."

"If you become a sailboat and sail away from me," said his mother, "I will become the wind and blow you where I want you to go."

"If you become the wind and blow me," said the little bunny, "I will join a circus and fly away on a flying trapeze."

"If you go flying on a flying trapeze," said his mother, "I will be a tightrope walker, and I will walk across the air to you."

"If you become a tightrope walker and walk across the air," said the bunny, "I will become a little boy and run into a house."

"If you become a little boy and run into a house," said the mother bunny, "I will become your mother and catch you in my arms and hug you."

7

"Shucks," said the bunny, "I might just as well stay where I am and be your little bunny."

And so he did.

"Have a carrot," said the mother bunny.

MRS. GOOSE'S BATH

by MIRIAM CLARK POTTER

One evening Mrs. Goose said to herself, "I think I'll take a nice bath in my little green tub. I don't like water as well as my friends Three-Ducks do; no, indeed. I like better to wipe my feathers off with a damp cloth. But today I am going to take a good, warm bath, and get myself all wet."

So she got the little green bathtub off its nail on the wall, and put it in the middle of her kitchen floor. She filled the kettle with water, and put it on the stove. She got out two big soft towels, and a piece of pink soap, and her wrapper and slippers. Then she sat down to read the Animaltown paper. "When the water is warm," said Mrs. Goose to herself, "I will start my bath."

She read a story, and looked at some pictures. Then she suddenly remembered that the water must be warm. She ran over to the stove and, sure enough, the water was warm—just right for a bath.

"Now for it!" said Mrs. Goose to herself. She put the towels, and the soap, and her wrapper and slippers on a chair by the tub. Then she thought to herself that she had forgotten to get a wash-cloth.

So she rushed to the little linen cupboard and found a nice blue one, with a little flower embroi-

dered in the corner. She plopped back to her tub again, and got in, with the wash-cloth and the soap.

"The soap is here, and the wash-cloth is here," she whispered to herself, "but still this does not seem like a bath. I wonder what the matter is?"

She began to rub her feathers with the wash-cloth. "This is a funny bath," she said. "Something is wrong. Soap, wash-cloth, me; soap, wash-cloth, me; yes, we are all here, right in the tub. And yet still something is the matter."

Just then she heard a quacking outside, and she knew that Three-Ducks were going by on their way to market.

She jumped out of the tub, and ran over to the window. She stuck her long, funny neck out. "Ho, you!" she called. "Come in here, Three-Ducks, and tell me what is the matter with my bath! Something seems to be wrong."

Three-Ducks laughed. "You've probably forgotten the soap," they told her.

Mrs. Goose looked around, just to be sure, and then she said, "No, I haven't."

"Then you've forgotten the wash-cloth."

Mrs. Goose looked around again.

"No, I haven't. It is a blue one, with a flower embroidered in the corner."

"Well," said Three-Ducks, "we'll come in and look things over, and see what the matter is." So in they waddled.

There was the little green tub, in the middle of the kitchen floor. There was the wash-cloth, and the towels, and the wrapper, and the soap; and Mrs. Goose, waiting to be washed. And there was the teakettle, sizzling on the stove. "I got into the tub," Mrs. Goose told Three-Ducks, "and tried to take a bath, but nothing happened. Something was missing, but I do not know what."

Three-Ducks began to laugh. "Oh, Mrs. Goose," they said, "we knew that you were funny and forgettery, but we didn't know you were as funny as that!"

"What is the matter with my bath?" asked Mrs. Goose.

Three-Ducks were laughing so hard that they could hardly quack the answer. Then they said— "The water, Mrs. Goose! You've forgotten to pour the water into the tub!"

Mrs. Goose blinked her black eyes at the sizzling teakettle. Then she began to laugh, too, "Well, I knew it was something important," she said.

THE GROWING UP STORY
OF JONATHAN

by LILIAN MOORE

It was bedtime for Jonathan.

"What story shall it be tonight?" asked Jonathan's mama.

Jonathan climbed up in his mama's lap.

"Tell me my growing up story," he said.

"Why, Jonathan," said Mama surprised. "I told you that story last night!"

"Tell it again," said Jonathan. "It's the best story of all."

"All right then," said Mama.

"Well," she began, "once you were a tiny, tiny baby, just about so big," and Mama spread her hands apart just a wee bit. "You had no hair on your

14

little head, and not a single tooth in your little mouth. You took all your food from a bottle, and most of the time, you wore diapers—oh, so many, many diapers!"

"Millions and trillions of diapers?" asked Jonathan.

"That's the way it seemed," laughed Mama. "Off with one and on with the other all day long. And my, were you the hungry one. Eat, eat, eat! And my, were you the sleepy one! Sleep, sleep, sleep!"

"Sh, I'm asleep," said Jonathan and he closed his eyes, curled up like a baby, and pretended to be asleep. Then after a minute he said, "Tell about how I got bigger."

"Well," said Mama, "you just kept growing and growing. And one day you had your first taste of cereal from a spoon. Most of it got over your face and over your bib and over your mama. But some of it got inside of you and you smiled. That was to say you liked it. You see, you were still too small to say even a word—imagine! not even one word—but you made all kinds of funny happy noises like 'ba-ba' and 'ooh-goo-ooh.' Sometimes you said 'da-da' and Daddy was so excited because he thought you were talking to him!"

"Da-da," said Jonathan, "I can't talk. Ba-ba. Da-da."

Mama and Jonathan both laughed, and then Mama said, "One day while you were making your funny happy noises, Daddy and I looked into your mouth and what do you think we saw?"

"A tooth!" cried Jonathan. "My first tooth!"

"That's right. Your very first tooth," and Mama put her finger on Jonathan's big front tooth. "There's the very tooth," she said.

"Tell me some more," said Jonathan, wiggling in

16

his mama's lap. "Tell me more about how I got to be bigger."

"Well, do you know, pretty soon it was time to make a little cake and put one candle in the middle of it—"

"My first birthday cake!" said Jonathan. "It had chocolate on it! Didn't it, Mama?"

"Yes, it did," said Mama, "and the first thing you did with that chocolate icing was to smear it with your fingers all over your face and your nice new suit. And then you looked so pleased with yourself, like little Jack Horner! You were still too little to talk, but my goodness, how fast you got around! Mostly on your hands and feet, of course, but faster than I could chase after you."

"Like this, Mama?" asked Jonathan, and he began to creep around the room, frontward and backward, on his hands and feet.

"Yes," said Mama, laughing. "Just like that!"

Then Jonathan stopped pretending to be one year old. He climbed back on his mama's lap.

"Tell about that picture," he said pointing to a picture in a frame on the table. It was the picture of a little boy with his teddy bear and his wagon.

"By the time we took that picture," said Mama,

17

"you could walk by yourself, and you could pull your little red wagon wherever you liked."

"That's Bo-Bo in the wagon," said Jonathan, looking at the picture. "And there's Bo-Bo now." Jonathan pointed to the shelf where his old teddy bear was sitting.

"You haven't played with him for a long time," said Mama, "but when you were little you wanted him to go everywhere with you. You used to say, 'Come bye-bye, Bo-Bo.' And every night you took him to sleep with you."

"Poor old Bo-Bo," said Jonathan. He ran over and patted his old teddy bear. "I bet he's lonesome. Maybe I'll let him sleep with me tonight."

"You took Bo-Bo with you the day you went to the barber for your very first haircut."

"I was afraid, wasn't I?" asked Jonathan.

"You certainly were," said his mama. "You cried and cried and even when the nice barber gave you a lollipop you were still very angry with him."

"Gosh," said Jonathan. "Why was I crying about a haircut?"

"You were frightened because you were so little. Do you know what else you were afraid of? The vacuum cleaner! When I turned it on, it made such a loud noise that you began to cry. But you were getting bigger all the time and one day, do you know what you did? You pushed the vacuum cleaner all around the room by yourself. You said you wanted to help Mama clean up."

"I guess I wasn't afraid of that old vacuum cleaner any more, was I?" asked Jonathan.

"No," said Mama, "and pretty soon after that you weren't afraid of the barber any more either.

When he gave you your next haircut, you were two years old. He gave you a peppermint lollipop and this time you said 'Thank you.' "

"That's 'cause I was big now, wasn't I?"

Mama laughed, "Bigger, yes, but not so very big. No diapers now. Real pants! And you could undress yourself pretty well by now. But what a tangle you made getting things on! You would stick both feet in one pants' leg, and then you got angry. You wouldn't let me help you either! You kept saying 'Me do it! Me do it!' "

"Me do it!" said Jonathan. "Look, Mama!" and he put his bedroom slippers on the wrong feet, just for fun.

"And then one day," Mama went on— "Guess what? One, two, three candles on a cake and—"

"Happy birthday to me!" cried Jonathan. "Tell me about when I was three. I was a good runner, wasn't I?"

"Oh, yes," said Mama. "My, the things you could do when you were three—run and jump, and even gallop like a little pony. And when you were three you got your new red tricycle. At first you made it go backward, mostly, but soon you were able to ride all the way to the super market with me!"

"And I could go real fast, couldn't I?" asked Jonathan. Then he gave a wiggle and said, "Now hurry up and tell about when I was four. I had a real birthday party didn't I, Mama? With cake

and ice cream, and Janey came and Andy and Tommy, too. Didn't they?"

"Yes, indeed," said Mama, "and pretty soon I'm going to make another birthday cake—with *five* candles on it. That's going to be for a big little boy who sleeps in a big bed now. My, my! just look what's happened to the little baby who couldn't eat from anything but a bottle, and who wore trillions of diapers! He grew and grew and grew—and soon he'll be five years old!"

"Then I'll be finished, won't I, Mama?" asked Jonathan.

Mama laughed and gave Jonathan a specially big hug. "No," she said. "Then you'll go on growing and growing and growing until some day you'll be a man just like Daddy!"

WHEN I GROW UP

by IRMA SIMONTON BLACK

When I grow up and I travel far
I won't go by truck and I won't go by car,
I won't go by boat and I won't go by train,
I'll drive through the sky in a big shiny plane.

I'll look down at houses, I'll look down at people,
I'll even look down on the pointy church steeple.
I'll look down at bees and beetles and bats,
I'll look down at sparrows and arrows and cats.

I'll go farther than far and faster than fast,
And you will look up when you hear me whiz past.
THAT'S what I'll do as soon as I'm grown
I'll get an airplane and have wings of my own!

LITTLE BEAR TAKES HIS NAP

by CATHERINE WOOLLEY

One morning when Little Bear went out to play in the woods, he found the air chilly. On the ground were patches of something wet and white that sparkled in the sun.

Just then Little Bear heard his mother calling.

"Come, Little Bear," called Mother Bear. "There is white frost on the ground. Winter is coming. Time for little bears to come in for their long winter nap."

Little Bear was scuffling in heaps of crackly red leaves. He was turning somersaults in them. The dusty leaves tickled his nose and made him sneeze. That was fun. He didn't want to take his long winter nap.

"No," said Little Bear to Mother Bear.

After a while Little Bear felt something wet on his little black nose. He looked up in surprise. Pretty white flakes were drifting and floating in the cold gray air.

"Come, Little Bear!" Mother Bear called. "The snow is falling. Winter is coming. Come in this minute for your long winter nap."

Little Bear was trying to catch the snowflakes with his paws. Every time he caught a snowflake it melted right away on his warm fur. That was funny! Little Bear didn't want to take his long winter nap.

"Pretty soon," said Little Bear to Mother Bear.

After a while Little Bear heard Mother Bear calling again.

"Good-by," Mother Bear called. "I'm going home for *my* long winter nap. You stay and play in the snow."

Little Bear stopped playing and looked around.

He watched Mother Bear go lumbering off toward home.

Little Bear didn't want to stay out in the woods alone.

Suddenly he thought how funny it would be to fool Mother Bear.

He turned softly around. He tiptoed after her, very quietly.

When Mother Bear got to the door of the bear house, Little Bear heard her talking to herself.

"I'm going in the house," said Mother Bear. "I'm going to shut the door. If Little Bear comes home he won't be able to get in. That will teach him a lesson!"

Little Bear put his paw over his mouth to keep from giggling. He was right behind Mother Bear. He slipped in the door.

Mother Bear closed the door.

"There!" said Mother Bear to herself. Now that Little Bear can just stay out all winter!"

Mother Bear lighted the lamp. She took down Little Bear's pajamas from a hook on the wall.

"Little Bear won't need his pajamas this winter,"
Mother Bear said to herself. "I'll just put them on
the bed while I get my nightie." Mother Bear
put her nightie on.

Little Bear reached out quietly and took his pajamas.

He put them on.

Mother Bear never noticed.

"Now," said Mother Bear, "I'll get in my warm
bed. I wonder if Little Bear is cold out there."

She climbed into bed.

Little Bear climbed in very softly next to Mother
Bear's back.

"What is tickling my back?" said Mother Bear.
"Must be a mosquito in here!"

She flapped her paw at the mosquito.

Little Bear held his breath so he wouldn't laugh.

He wiggled closer to Mother Bear.

"There is some animal in my bed!" said Mother
Bear. "I'm going to find out what!"

She reached her paw back and felt of Little Bear's
ears.

Little Bear was still as a mouse.

"Hm," said Mother Bear.

She felt of Little Bear's snout.

"My goodness!" said Mother Bear.

She felt of Little Bear's little fat tummie.

And she tickled!

The giggles burst right out of Little Bear!

He doubled up his little feet and he waved his little paws and he squealed and laughed and giggled.

Mother Bear was so surprised she nearly fell out of bed.

"For goodness', gracious' sake!" gasped Mother Bear. "How in the world did you get here?"

"I fooled you!" squealed Little Bear, laughing till the tears almost rolled down his cheeks.

"Dear me!" said Mother Bear.

Little Bear gave a deep sigh of joy to think he had fooled Mother Bear.

Then he yawned.

He snuggled a little closer.

He went to sleep for his long winter nap.

SANDY GOES TO THE CIRCUS

by DOROTHY SHERRILL

Sandy Macdonald sat tied to a gatepost,
   Sandy Macdonald was sad.
All of the children had gone to the circus;
   Sandy Macdonald felt bad.

"There'll be bears at the circus,"
   Said Sandy Macdonald;
"Big bears to bark at, and lions that roar.
   I want to see lions!"
   Cried Sandy Macdonald.
"I don't want to sit here tied up any more!"

Sandy Macdonald broke loose from the gatepost,
   Sandy Macdonald was free!
He ran all the way from his home to the circus;
   A very fine runner was he.

There were bears at the circus,
    And monkeys and zebras,
And elephants dancing and beating a drum.
    The lions were lovely,
    The elephants gorgeous.
And Sandy was terribly glad he had come.

Sandy Macdonald liked all of the circus.
    Especially the seals that did tricks.
If only he hadn't espied the balloon man,
    He'd never have got in a fix.

The balloon man was hungry,
    'Twas time to be eating.
He tied his balloons down and went for his lunch.
    Along came young Sandy,
    His eyes full of mischief;
He untied the knot and took hold of the bunch.

Sandy Macdonald went up like a rocket,
  Up like a bird in the air!
The clowns in the circus all cried to each other,
  "Oh see the black doggie up there!"

The children saw Sandy,
  The children were frightened.

"Oh please save our doggie!" they begged of a clown.
   "Sure thing," said he kindly,
   "I'll fly in my airplane,
In less than three minutes I'll bring your dog down."

   Sandy was tired of holding balloon strings,
     Yet didn't quite dare let them go.
The clown in the airplane flew right up beneath him
     And pulled Sandy in by the toe!

Now Sandy Macdonald stays home when he's told
     to;
   A much wiser doggie is he.
   "Let birds do the flying!"
    Says Sandy Macdonald,
    "BUT NO MORE BALLOON RIDES FOR
      ME!"

THE HORSE WHO LIVED UPSTAIRS

by PHYLLIS MCGINLEY

There was once a horse named Joey who was discontented.

He was discontented because he didn't live in a red barn with a weathervane on top, and he didn't live in a green meadow where he could run about and kick up his heels.

Instead, he lived upstairs in a big brick building in New York.

Joey worked for Mr. Polaski who sold fruits and vegetables to city people.

Joey pulled the vegetable wagon through the city streets.

And in New York, there isn't room for barns or meadows.

So every night when Joey came home, he stepped out from the shafts of the wagon, and into an elevator, and up he went to his stall on the fourth floor of the big brick building. It was a fine stall and Joey was very comfortable there. He had plenty of oats to eat and plenty of fresh straw to lie on.

He even had a window to look out of.

But still Joey was discontented.

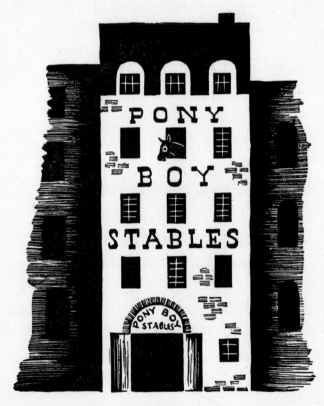

"How I long to sip fresh water from a babbling brook!" he often exclaimed.

And then he would sniff discontentedly at the old bathtub near the elevator which served him as a watering trough.

It wasn't that he had to work hard. Mr. Polaski was kind to him and brought him home at five o'clock every day.

In the winter Joey had a blanket to wear on his back to keep him warm.

And in the summer time Mr. Polaski got him a hat to wear on his head to keep him cool.

And every day he had many interesting adventures. Sometimes he met a Policeman who gave him sugar.

Sometimes ladies patted him on the nose and fed him carrots.

He was introduced to the high-bred horses who drew the hansom cabs along the Plaza.

He saw the children playing in the playgrounds and the parks.

But it made no difference to Joey. "This is no life for a horse," he used to say to the Percheron who lived in the next stall to him. "We city horses don't know what real living is. I want to move to the country and sleep in a red barn with a weathervane on top, and kick up my heels in a green meadow."

So how happy he was when one day Mr. Polaski said to him, "Joey, I think I could sell more vegetables if I drove a truck. I will miss you, Joey, but you will like it on the farm where I am going to send you."

The next morning a big motor van rolled up. Joey got inside, and away he went to the country. Of course he said good-by to the Percheron. "Good-by, Joey," called his friend. "I hope you will be contented on the farm."

When Joey reached the country, sure enough, there was the barn with its weathervane, and there was the meadow.

"This is the life!" cried Joey to himself.

But poor Joey!

The barn was cold in winter and hot in summer. He didn't have a blanket and he didn't have a hat. And he had very little time to kick up his heels in the green meadow, for all day long he pulled a plow through the earth.

A plow is harder to pull than a wagon, and besides, the farmer worked from sunrise to sundown instead of the eight hours Joey was used to.

Sometimes they forgot to put fresh straw in his stall, and nobody thought to give him sugar or carrots.

There were plenty of children but they climbed on his back and teased him when he wanted to eat. And instead of the Percheron, there was a cross old gray horse next door to him, who looked down his nose at Joey because Joey knew so little about farm life.

One day, when he wasn't pulling a plow, because it was Sunday, Joey saw several people picnicking in the meadow. He decided to join them, for they looked as if they came from the City, and he thought they might have a lump of sugar in one of their pockets.

When he reached the spot they had gone for a walk, so he ate up their lunch.

When they came back, they were very angry and Joey was shut up in his stall for the rest of the day. He didn't even have a window to look out of.

He was lonely for his friends, the Policeman, and the ladies who patted him on the nose.

He was lonely for the high-bred horses, and all the interesting sights of the City.

"I don't think I belong in the country after all," sighed Joey. "I am now more discontented than ever."

Next day he heard the honk of a horn. He looked from the door of the barn, and whom should he see but Mr. Polaski, getting out of the truck!

"I have come for Joey," Mr. Polaski told the farmer. "I cannot get any more tires for my truck, so I think I will sell fruit and vegetables from my wagon again."

My goodness, but Joey was happy!

He went back to the City with Mr. Polaski and got into the elevator and up he went to the fourth floor of the big brick building. There was his stall, and there was the window for him to look out of.

And there was the friendly Percheron.

"Welcome back, Joey," exclaimed the Percheron. "I have missed you. The Policeman has missed you. The lady customers have missed you, and so have the children in the playgrounds and the parks. Tell me, how did you like the country?"

"The country is all right for country animals," Joey said, "but I guess I am just a City horse at heart."

And he was never discontented again.

TUM-TE-TUM, HERE WE COME!

by LEONE ADELSON

Johnny marched down the street and beat his new drum.

Tum-te-tum went the drum.

And Johnny shouted, "Here I come!"

He marched past his house, and past the house next door, and there was Penny on her front doorstep.

"Where are you going with your drum?" she wanted to know.

"I'm having a parade and you can come," Johnny answered.

"Can I bring my doll?" asked Penny.

"Oh, yes, you can," said Johnny.

And off they marched.

Johnny's drum went tum-te-tum.

And there was Bill who wanted to come.

"Wait for me, I'll get my jeep," said Billy.

And he rode his jeep at the end of the parade.

Beep! Beep! went the jeep.

"Jeepers!" said Johnny. "My parade is getting bigger!"

. One, two, three, four,

Tramp, tramp, stamp, stamp,

Beep! Beep! Tum-te-tum, tum-te-tum.

42

"We're having a parade and you can come!"
Johnny shouted to Suzie when they came to her
house.

"Can I bring my baby brother?" Suzie asked.

"Sure!" said Johnny. "He can come too."

Soon they came to Helen's house. Helen was
looking out of the window.

"We're having a parade—do you want to come?"
Johnny called.

"Yes, I do," said Helen, "but I have the measles."

"Then you can't come," said Johnny.

And on they went,

March, march, one two,

Stamp, stamp, three four,

What a big parade behind Johnny's drum!

Then they came to Tommy's house, and there was
Tommy.

"Golly! A parade!" he cried. "Can I come on my
bike?"

"Yes," said Johnny. "Ride your bike and ring your
bell."

So Tommy came on his bike, ringing his bell—
dr-r-ring, dr-r-ring, ting-a-ling.

And then the twins joined the parade with their
rattley red express wagon.

And after that, Sammy the dog came, with his flap-

43

ping red tongue. The drum beat, and Sammy barked.

WRUF-WRUF

TUM TUM, tum te tum.

Johnny's parade was very long now.

Straight down the street they marched—right to the corner.

The policeman stopped the cars to let them cross.

"That's a fine parade you have there!" he called after them.

Stamp-stamp, march-march they went, past all the big stores on the big street. The people came running out of the stores to see what the noise was all about.

The shoemaker in his black apron came out to watch; and the man whose shoe he was fixing came out with one shoe off and one shoe on.

44

The barber came to the door to see what was going on, and the man he was shaving looked out of the window with soap all over his face.

Everyone smiled and waved. It was such a fine parade that Johnny decided to take it home and show it to his mother.

"All right, now," he called out. "Everybody march back to my house!"

They marched back across the street.

But when they came to the twins' house, there was the twins' mother calling them for lunch.

They didn't want to leave the parade, but they were hungry, so they went. Now the parade had no rattley wagon.

Johnny's drum beat very fast—TUMtumTUM-tumTUMtumTUMtum.

He wanted to hurry the parade along to his house. But when they got to Tommy's house, he had to go in for lunch, too.

Now the parade had no ting-a-ling bike bell.

"Gosh," said Johnny. Hurry up or we'll never get to my house."

And he beat his drum as fast as he possibly could—tumtumtumtum—but it was no use.

Suzie's baby brother began to cry, so they went home, too.

45

"Left - right - forward - march - hurry - up!" said Johnny, crossly.

But it didn't help at all, because Billy was hungry, too. When they came to his house, he rode his jeep right up to his front door.

Beep-beep! No more jeep!

"Oh, please wait till we get to my house," Johnny said to Penny, but Penny was tired, and she went home, too.

Now there was only Sammy the dog, and Johnny and his drum.

Tum-te-tum.

WRUF-WRUF!

But just then a cat ran by, and Sammy had to chase after the cat!

Johnny was all alone. The parade he wanted to show his mother was all gone. There was no one to beat his drum for.

Johnny felt very sad. He didn't even see a car stop at the curb.

His father was home for lunch. He ran up to Johnny and swung him high in the air.

"Well-well-well-well!" he cried. "Johnny, you led the best parade this town has ever seen! I saw it from my office window, every bit of it—even when the policeman stopped the traffic."

"But, Daddy, they all went home!" Johnny wailed.

His father laughed. "Of course," he said. "It's lunchtime."

"I wanted Mommy to see it," Johnny said, "and now there's nothing to see."

"But there's lots to tell," said his daddy. "Let's go and tell Mommy all about it."

"All right!" Johnny shouted. "Come on, Daddy, forward–MARCH!"

And Johnny and his daddy marched up the front steps.

Stamp-stamp went their feet.

TUM TUM went the drum.

    Tum te tum . . .

    . . . te tum. . . .

    . . . . . te tum . . .

TUM!

HOUSES

by JESSIE ORTON JONES

How could God think of so many kinds of houses?
There are millions of houses that I can't even see.
There must be lots of very funny ones!
    Mole houses—
        Frog houses—
            Beaver houses—
Stork nests on chimneys,
Squirrel nests in trees.
Houses for everyone!
    And my house
        For me.

THE STORY OF A LITTLE
GRAY MOUSE

by DOROTHY SHERRILL

Once upon a time there was a little gray mouse.

He lived with his mother and father and nine brothers and sisters in a funny little house in an attic. The house was really an old hatbox with a hat on top of it and a chimney sticking out of the hat.

One day the mother mouse said to the little mice, "Children, now that you are all growing up and aren't tiny baby mice any longer, this hatbox is getting very crowded. The time has come for you to go out into the world and find homes of your own."

And the father mouse, who had been reading his newspaper while the mother mouse was talking, put it down now and said to them, "Your mother is right. You are almost grown-up and must go find homes of your own. Good-by, be good little mice." And he patted them on their little gray heads.

So the children packed their toys and a clean necktie and a piece of cheese in a handkerchief, and they said good-by in their squeaky little voices. They promised to be good mice; and off they scampered to find homes of their own.

Now the little mouse that we are telling this story about ran outdoors with the others. But when he got outside he just couldn't decide where he wanted to live.

He walked very slowly down the road carrying his handkerchief bundle over his shoulder.

Bye and bye he came to a pond that had lots of beautiful water-lilies in it. He sat down beside the pond to rest. And a big grandfather frog, who was perched on a log, said to him, "Gur-runk, gur-runk!" which is the way a frog says, "Where are you going, little mouse?"

When the little mouse told him that he was looking for a place to live, the old frog was very polite.

"Come here and live with me on this nice big brown log," he said.

"Thank you, I will," said the little mouse. And he jumped quickly from the shore to the log. But when he got on the log he didn't like it at all. It wobbled every time he moved, and it was very, very wet.

So the little mouse said politely to the old frog, "Thank you, but I don't really think logs are very good places for mice to live, although they may be lovely for frogs." And he jumped quickly back on to dry land and scampered down the road.

The little mouse ran and ran until he came under a big tree and heard a bird say, "Chirp, chirp, chirpee!" which is the way a bird says, "Where are you going, little mouse?"

When the little mouse told the bird that he was looking for a place to live, the bird said politely, "Won't you come and live with me in my tree?"

"Thank you, I'd like to," said the little mouse. And he climbed up the tree.

But when the little mouse got into the tree, and night came and the wind blew and the tree rocked, he didn't like it at all. He wished he were back in his quiet home in the attic.

"Thank you," the little mouse whispered very softly so as not to wake up the bird who was sleeping soundly. "Nests in trees may be very nice for birds," he said, "but they're not very nice for me!" So he climbed down the tree and ran away.

He slept under a big stone that night. And in the morning, after eating some cheese for breakfast, he began to walk along the road again. Pretty soon he came to a sign that read, "This Way to the City."

"Goody!" he said out loud in his squeaky little voice. "I'll go to the city. Maybe I will find a place to live there." So he walked very fast until he came to the big buildings of the city. They looked awfully big to him. "Gracious me!" he squeaked. "Wouldn't it be terrible if they toppled over on me!"

And he began to feel very little and lonely.

Just then he saw a cellar doorway. It was open and the cellar looked nice and warm and safe inside. "I think I'll go in there and build a nest," said the little mouse. So he went in and closed the door behind him.

It was very nice in the cellar and the little mouse was pleased with it. He hunted around for some old rags and wood shavings and began to build a nest in a warm dark corner.

He was so very busy building his nest that he didn't see a pussy cat that came crawling toward him out of the coal bin.

The little mouse went right on building, and kitty came nearer and nearer. Until what do you think happened? Pussy stepped on a piece of coal that rolled over and made a noise! And the mouse heard it! He looked around and saw the cat's big green eyes glaring at him.

The mouse jumped straight up in the air! Kitty jumped too, but missed him. "Mercy!" squeaked the little mouse, "I won't stay here!"

"Yes you will!" Pussy cried.

"No I won't!" squeaked the mouse, running to the door and slipping safely out through a hole under it.

Of course, the kitty was too big to go through the hole.

So the little mouse got away and ran as fast as ever he could down the street.

He ran right out of the city, past the big tree where the bird lived, past the pond where the frog was. He ran and ran until he came to the house that had the attic where his mother and father lived.

He was so happy to see it again that he said, "Why

did I try to go so far away from home to find a place to live? I can build myself a fine nest in a corner of that big attic right near my mother and father!"

And what do you think he saw when he got there? His nine brothers and sisters—who hadn't been able to find any other place they liked for a home either— all building nests in different parts of the attic!

Those little mice were so glad to be together again

that they all took hands and danced round and round
in a circle with their father and mother in the middle.
And after their dance they had a fine picnic on
bread and cheese. And they never left their home
again.

900 BUCKETS OF PAINT

by EDNA BECKER

Once there was an Old Woman who lived in a little red house that stood beside a laughing brook, right
in the middle of a field of clover. With her lived her
two cats, Pansy and Violet, and her donkey, whose
name was Arthur, and her cow, Bossy.

The Old Woman's house had once been a very
bright red. But the sun and wind and rain had beaten
against it until it was faded and worn. One day the
Old Woman decided that it looked too shabby to live
in any longer. So she decided to move.

She began packing early the next morning. By noon she had all her belongings loaded into the donkey's cart. All, that is, but her alarm clock. She set this inside the cupboard with glass doors until it was time to start. Then she brought the cats down from the attic.

The Old Woman hitched the donkey to the cart and tied the cow behind. Then she climbed up onto the seat of the donkey cart.

She put Pansy on one side of her and Violet on the other. And off she drove, forgetting all about her clock.

When the Old Woman reached the first corner, she turned to the right. Then she kept on going straight ahead until at last, far down the road, she spied a little yellow house all freshly painted.

"I think I'd like to live here," she said to herself as she drove into the yard.

She tied Arthur to a post and went to see if anybody lived there. Nobody did, so she set about at once unpacking her belongings. By evening she was nicely settled.

The next morning the Old Woman overslept dreadfully, not having her alarm clock. Just the same, when she woke she felt very well satisfied with herself.

"How do you like it here?" she asked Pansy and Violet.

The cats waved their long tails. "Meow," they said. "Fine. There are plenty of mice in the attic."

After breakfast the Old Woman went out to milk the cow.

"How do you like it here, Bossy?" she asked.

Bossy rolled her big brown eyes. "Moo!" she said. "Very much indeed. The clover is sweet and tender, and there is plenty of it."

The Old Woman, feeling very happy, went to give the donkey a bucket of water.

"How do you like it here, Arthur?" she asked.

"Hee, haw!" brayed Arthur. "I think it is terrible!"

"Why, Arthur!" cried the Old Woman. "What is wrong?"

"I won't drink out of a bucket, so there!" said
Arthur. And he stamped his foot.

"Why, what is the matter with a nice clean
bucket?" asked the Old Woman.

"I want to drink out of a laughing brook," stormed
Arthur. And he would not drink out of the bucket.

All the next day Arthur grumbled and complained.

At last the Old Woman packed up her belongings
and set out to find a house that had a laughing brook
for the donkey to drink from.

When she reached the first corner, she turned to
the right. Then she kept on going straight ahead
until at last, far down the road, she spied a little
bright green house.

A laughing brook ran close by.

"I think I'd like to live here," she said to herself.
Nobody lived in the house, so the Old Woman set

about at once unpacking her belongings. She found the house very comfortable.

The next morning Pansy and Violet were merrily running around in the attic, catching mice. Arthur was down at the brook, drinking. The Old Woman, feeling very happy, went to milk the cow. But Bossy would not give her any milk.

"Why, Bossy!" scolded the Old Woman. "What is the matter?"

"Mmm," moaned Bossy. "I don't like it here. There isn't enough clover."

"I will get you some hay," the Old Woman promised.

"I don't want hay. I want clover," grumbled Bossy.

"What shall I do?" sighed the Old Woman. "I'll just have to move again."

The next morning the Old Woman packed up and set out to find a house that had a brook and a clover field, too. She sighed and she drove away, for she liked the little green house.

When the Old Woman reached the first corner she turned to the right. Then she kept on going straight ahead until at last, far down the road, she spied a little low-roofed house. She didn't like the house very well, but there was a laughing brook beside it and a field of clover around it. Nobody lived there, so the Old Woman set about at once unpacking her belongings.

The next morning after breakfast the Old Woman went out to milk the cow. Bossy was nibbling contentedly at the clover. Arthur was down by the brook.

The Old Woman carried back to the house the brimming bucketful of milk Bossy had given her and poured out a big saucerful for Pansy and Violet.

"Here, kitties!" she called.

"Here, kitties!"

But Pansy and Violet did not come. At last the Old Woman found the cats, sulking in a corner.

"For gracious' sake," she said. "What is the matter?"

"Meow, meow!" whined Pansy and Violet. "There isn't any attic in this house and we can't find any mice. We won't live here."

The Old Woman rushed from one room to the other, trying to find a way to the attic. But the cats were right. There wasn't any attic.

"Whatever shall I do?" she sighed.

There was nothing for her to do but to pack up and move once more.

She started out the next morning. When she reached the first corner, the Old Woman turned to the right. Then she kept on going straight ahead for a long, long way. At last, far down the road, the Old Woman spied a little white house. There was a clover field around it, and it looked high enough to have an attic.

"Now if there is only a brook," the Old Woman said to herself.

Just then the wheels of her cart rumbled over a little bridge, and there was the brook.

"This is the very place for us!" she thought as she drove into the yard.

As she was getting out of the cart, a man came

63

around the corner of the house with a paint bucket in his hand. The Old Woman's heart sank.

"Do you live here?" she asked.

"Oh, no," replied the man cheerfully. "I've just been painting the house. You see, a man gave me nine hundred buckets of paint. I wasn't very busy, so I thought I'd paint all the houses around here that looked shabby. It will make things look much better."

"That is certainly kind of you," replied the Old Woman. "Will it be all right for me to move in here with my two cats, my donkey, and my cow?"

"Certainly, certainly," said the painter. "Move right in. I'll finish the fence, then I'll be leaving."

The Old Woman began unpacking. As she put some plates into the cupboard with glass doors, she saw something that surprised her very much. It was an alarm clock.

The Old Woman took it out and looked at it carefully.

"Well, I declare," she said at last. "I do believe this is my own clock. I remember now that I forgot it when I moved the first time. I wonder . . ."

The Old Woman went to the door.

"Oh, Mr. Painter!" she called out. "Do you happen to remember what color this house was before you painted it white?"

"It was red," the painter shouted back. "But it was very old and faded. That's why I painted it."

"Well, I declare!" said the Old Woman again. "Well, it was a nice vacation!"

PARK PLAY

by JAMES S. TIPPETT

Every morning
I can play
In the park
Across the way.

I can run
And I can shout.
I am glad
When I come out.

66

TAMMIE AND THAT PUPPY

by DOROTHY *and* MARGUERITE BRYAN

One day when Tammie the little Scottie dog was at the front gate, waiting for his friend, the postman, he heard a call. He listened— Yes, someone was calling from the back of the house. "Here Tammie, here Tammie, come Tammie!"

Tammie started on a trot around the house.

"Hurry Tammie! Surprise, SURPRISE! Here Tammie!"

A surprise might be so many things—good things that Tammie liked. It might be something to eat. Tammie trotted faster. Or it might be a game of ball. Tammie began to run. Or a picnic! Tammie ran as fast as he could until he found Sally, Peter and little George, all looking at something in Sally's arms.

Tammie ran round and round, trying to find out what Sally had for a surprise.

Finally he sat up and stretched until he could see —It was a puppy!

Sally put the puppy on the ground. It was little and fat and black—a Scottie like Tammie.

"Look Tammie," Sally said. "This darling puppy has come to stay with us. His name is Bobby."

Tammie sat and looked at Bobby— Then he turned and walked away, all by himself.

He was cross—he wanted a ball or a picnic—*not* a puppy.

Everybody making such a fuss about that silly puppy!

Bobby scampered over and, taking the tip of Tammie's ear in his sharp little teeth, pulled and pulled. Tammie growled and pushed him away, rolling him onto his back. Bobby squealed—"Yip-Yip-Yip!"

The children all hurried to comfort him.

"Why Tammie," Peter scolded, "aren't you ashamed of yourself?"

"Poor little puppy, don't cry," Sally coaxed.

"Bad dog," said little George.

Tammie turned his back. He was *very* cross now.

THAT PUPPY!

He decided to go and chew for a while on his nice big bone.

He had just started to enjoy himself when Bobby pranced up and began tugging, with small growls, at one end of *his*, Tammie's, own bone. Never had such a thing happened before!

Tammie dropped the bone and walked away.

He went to his eating dish. He had left a little of his breakfast. It might make him feel more cheerful to finish it up now.

His dish was empty! Someone had been there before him! THAT PUPPY!!

Never had such a thing happened before!

Tammie marched to his favorite chair—the chair that was always left for him.

There, in the center of his cushion, sat THAT
PUPPY.

Never, *never* had such a thing happened before!

Tammie went over to the garage and crawled
under the car. What to do?

He lay there for a long time—then he started off
down the road.

He was going to find a new home where there
were not any puppies about.

He disappeared over the top of the hill.

He went to the meat store. He would stay there.
The butcher was a jolly man and there would be
many meat scraps.

BUT—

the butcher's cat soon chased him away.

Tammie trotted in at the gate of the house where Joe lived with his big dog, Spot. He would stay with them. He heard Joe talking to Spot in the back yard, so went around there. As he turned the corner *what* did he see?

Joe was giving Spot a bath!

Tammie turned and rushed out through the gate. No bath for him!

He was panting when he met his dog friends, Michael and Patsy. They played together for a while and then, when it began to grow dark, Michael and Patsy started for home.

Tammie went with them. They were his friends and he would stay at their house.

Michael and Patsy and Tammie all tried to crowd on the sleeping cushion together. Michael was the most comfortable. Patsy next, and Tammie not comfortable at all.

Tammie went out onto the road. Everything was dark and quiet. No one was about—everyone at home. Tammie's eyes were big and shining in the dark.

Tammie was lonesome—he would go home to his own house.

What was that? He listened—
"Come Tammie!
Here Tammie!
Tammie!
Tammie!!
Tam-m-i-e-e-e! Please come home"—

He ran as fast as his legs would carry him and jumped right into the arms of the waiting children, who hugged him hard.

Even the puppy licked his face.

It was bedtime. Tammie watched to see. Yes, all was well. The puppy was left in a box downstairs while he, Tammie, went up the stairs and where *best* loved dogs can always be found
THERE WAS TAMMIE!

RED MITTENS

by LAURA BANNON

"What are you making?" asked little Joe.

"It is a secret. You have to guess," answered Mommie. She smiled as she knit and knit and knit.

"Red mittens!" cried little Joe.

"Yes, a pair of red mittens for you," said Mommie.

"Hold still," said little Joe's Mommie. She slipped some red yarn over his hands and began winding the end into a little ball. The ball grew bigger and bigger until all the yarn was wound onto it. Then Mommie began to knit with four needles.

When they were finished, she put some fancy black stitches on the back. Then she fastened them together with a long black crocheted string, so he wouldn't lose them.

Little Joe thought they were beautiful.

74

When the whirling snow came, it piled up in the meadow back of little Joe's house. Every hill looked like a big cake with white frosting.

The small animals that lived in the meadow stayed in their homes down under the ground to keep warm. But little Joe went out with his sled and made long lovely curves in the smooth snow frosting. His red mittens helped him stay warm as toast.

Little Joe liked his mittens so much he wore them all the time. When summer came, it was too warm to keep them on his hands. So he wound the string around his neck and wore them on the front of his overalls for carrying things.

The cows were let out of the barn to eat the green grass. Small animals scampered about again in the warm sunshine. They were all little Joe's

75

friends and he had long talks with them when he
played in the meadow.

One day little Joe suddenly stopped playing. His
mittens! Where were they?

They were not on the front of his overalls.

They were not in his pockets.

They were not anywhere on the ground.

They were lost. Poor little Joe!

Little Joe couldn't be happy without his mittens.
He wandered about looking for them.

A kind hen was scratching for worms among the
milkweeds.

"I have lost my beautiful red mittens," little Joe
told her.

"Where did you lose them?" asked the hen.

"Somewhere in the meadow," said little Joe. He
wanted to cry.

"Don't be sad," said the kind hen. "I have very sharp eyes. I will help you find them."

And so the hen and little Joe looked for the mittens.

They were not around the prickly thistle bushes.

They were not under the big toadstools.

They were not among the tall cat-tails in the marsh where little Joe had been trying to catch frogs.

The red mittens were gone! Little Joe had big tears in his eyes.

"What are you looking for?" asked a friendly pussy cat who was hunting for field mice in the tall ferns.

"Little Joe has lost his mittens," said the hen.

"My beautiful red mittens!" added little Joe.

"We have looked all over the ground for them."

"You just looked on the ground!" exclaimed the friendly cat. "You should look *high* and *low* for them. I have eyes that can see even in the dark. I will help you find them."

The cat and the hen and little Joe looked *high* and *low*.

Little Joe looked *high*.
They were not on top of the tall bushes.
They were not in the trees.
The hen and the cat looked *low*.
They were not under the big leaves.
They were not in the patch of dandelions.
Poor little Joe began to cry.
By an old stump they met a wide-awake cow.

"Did you lose something?" asked the cow.

Little Joe nodded his head. He had a lump in his throat.

"He lost his red mittens," said the hen.

"And we have looked *high* and *low* for them," said the cat.

"You just looked *high* and *low* for them!" exclaimed the wide-awake cow. "You should look *high* and *low* and in the *middle*. I have such big eyes for looking. I will help you find them."

The hen, the cat, the cow and little Joe looked for the mittens.

Little Joe looked *high*.

The cat and the hen looked *low*.

And the cow looked in the *middle*.

They looked everywhere in the meadow.

The mittens were not in the robin's nest in the oak.

They were not in the rabbit's hole at its roots.

They were not in the old shoe the cat found in the tall grass.

Suddenly the cow started to laugh.

She giggled and laughed and laughed and giggled.

Little Joe was surprised.

So were the hen and the cat.

"When a beautiful pair of red mittens is lost, it is not something to laugh about," said the kind hen.

"And it is not good manners," said little Joe.

"But I have found your mittens," cried the wide-awake cow. "Ha! Ha! Ha! You will never guess where."

"They are not *high*," said little Joe.

"They are not *low*," said the cat.

"Where are they?" asked the hen.

"They are in the *middle*," said the cow.

"Show us the mittens," cried little Joe.

"I will show you the mittens if you do as I say," said the cow.

"You stand beside me," the cow said to the hen. The hen did.

"You stand on the other side of me," she said to the cat.

The cat did.

"Now, you stand in front of me," the cow said to little Joe.

Little Joe stood facing the cow.

"Now turn around," said the cow.

Little Joe turned around.

The hen and the cat and the cow laughed and laughed.

Little Joe did not laugh.

"I don't see my mittens," he said.

"Your mittens are in the middle of your back," the hen told him.

"Feel the string around your neck," said the friendly cat.

Little Joe felt the string around his neck. He pulled the beautiful red mittens to the front where

81

he could see them. How surprised he was to find they had been on his back all the time!

Little Joe was happy again. After that, whenever he met the kind hen or the friendly cat or the wide-awake cow in the meadow, they all had a good laugh about the time he lost his mittens.

RAIN

by MARY MC BURNEY GREEN

I like them all—
The different kinds of rain
That fall
Tap tapping on my roof.

Little creeping crawling rain
Wiggling down my window pane
Scarcely makes a sound.

Slanting dancing prancing rain
Bounces on the ground.

Hurry scurry flurry rain
With blowy windy sound.

I like them all
But best of all
I like to be
Tucked in my bed
All cozily
And listen to the rain
Tap tapping on my window pane.

THE SAILBOAT THAT RAN AWAY

by MADYE LEE CHASTAIN

Once there was a little toyshop that stood in the middle of a large city. All around it the city lived and moved. Trolley cars clanged to and fro. Automobiles honked their horns, subways rumbled underneath, and people hurried back and forth.

But inside the toyshop all was quiet. Well—*almost* quiet. Among the trucks and stuffed toys and engines with coal cars sat a little sailboat with a bright red hull and fine white sails. He looked very gay and jolly, but he felt sad and discontented.

"What a spot for a sailboat!" he grumbled. "Nothing but dusty streets and pavement everywhere. Not a spoonful of water in sight—much less enough to sail a boat in. Oh, if someone would only buy me and take me home! I'd show them what fun we could have!"

The days passed, and people came in to buy the other toys. But no one bought the sailboat.

Sometimes a little girl or boy would say, "Oh, what a beautiful sailboat!"

But the mothers would say, "You have no place to sail a boat. Let's buy a coal truck or a train."

Weeks and months went by and the little sailboat grew sadder and sadder. One day he felt *so* discouraged and *so* discontented that he said to himself, "I'm so very tired of this stuffy toyshop. If anyone ever does buy me, as soon as they put me in the water, I'll sail away! And I'll never come back! Yes, that's what I'll do—I'll go so fast they'll never catch me!"

Then one day Tommy's father came into the toyshop. You could see he was looking for something special.

The man passed by the trucks and wagons and stuffed toys and the engines with coal cars.

Suddenly he saw the little sailboat and he said, "That's what I want! That fine sailboat. That's just what I want for Tommy!"

The little sailboat was so surprised that one of his sails fell down—plop!

The man paid for him then and there and took him home—first on a bus—then on a train—all the way to the country.

When Tommy saw the sailboat he cried, "Oh, it's the most beautiful sailboat I ever saw."

This pleased the little sailboat because he had never before had anyone to love him. "But just the same," he thought, "when I get into the water, I'll sail away and I'll never come back!"

Tommy's father said, "Do you know—if we hurry—I think we'll have time to sail this boat a little while before dinner."

Tommy quickly wiped the dust off the boat's hull and his mother sewed the sail where it had come loose.

So Tommy and his father took the sailboat down to the lake near their home and they put him into the water.

A little breeze came by and filled the sails and away he went! It was a wonderful feeling—skimming along on the water! The little sailboat turned this way and that way. He caught the wind in his sails and sailed farther and farther away.

"Oh!" cried Tommy. "It's sailing too far away! It won't come back!"

"Indeed, I won't," thought the little sailboat and it felt very brave and carefree.

Just then a little silvery fish swam by.

"Hello, Sailboat! Where are you going?" asked the little fish.

"I'm running away," said the sailboat. "Where are you going?"

"Oh, I'm going home. It's getting dark," said the fish.

Then a dragonfly flew by and called, "Hello, Sailboat! Where are you going?"

"I'm running away," said the sailboat. "Where are you going?"

"Oh, I'm going home. It's getting late," said the dragonfly.

And the dragonfly hurried away.

A frog was sitting on a lily pad and it said, "Hello, Sailboat! Where are you going?"

"I'm running away. Where are you going?"

"I'm going home—this very minute!" said the frog.

And the frog plopped into the blue, blue water.

The little sailboat sailed on and on. But he began to notice that it was getting darker and darker and stiller and stiller. All the birds had flown to their nests. The frogs and fish had disappeared. All the little animals had left the shores of the lake and were safe at home with their families. Even the butterflies and bees had gone to their homes.

"Oh," thought the little sailboat. "It is getting late. Everyone has gone home. I'm all alone."

88

And he didn't know whether he liked that or not.

Suddenly he thought, "Why, I have a home, too —with the little boy who loves me! I can't run away from someone who loves me. I can't run away like this!"

The little sailboat turned about. He could see Tommy far away, waving his hands. Catching the wind in his sails, the little boat sailed straight for shore.

As he came closer he saw Tommy's face looking so bright and happy that he sailed even faster. When he came up to the shore, Tommy lifted the sailboat out of the water and he said to his father, "Now, we'll all go home together."

"Yes," thought the little sailboat happily. "We'll all go home together—and I'll never run away again —never!"

MR. ZOOLY'S ZOO

by MARGARET FARQUHAR

Mr. Zooly kept a very fine zoo.

He had monkeys and tigers and kangaroos.

He had lions and bears and elephants.

Every day, Mr. Zooly kept getting more animals until finally, he didn't have room for any more.

The animals were very well behaved. Everybody liked them except Mr. Crabshaw. He lived all by himself in a great big house next door to the zoo. The noise of the animals bothered Mr. Crabshaw. And he complained to Mr. Zooly about the noise.

Mr. Zooly tried to keep the animals quiet but he couldn't.

The lions roared. The bears growled.

The elephants trumpeted.

One day, Mr. Crabshaw came to call on Mr. Zooly.

"Mr. Zooly," said Mr. Crabshaw, "please keep your animals quiet. If you don't, I will have to report you to the police. It is against the LAW to disturb the peace, and your animals are disturbing MY peace. If I report you, the Chief of Police will make you send all the animals back to the countries they came from."

Then Mr. Crabshaw shook his cane very hard at Mr. Zooly and he went back to his great big house.

After that, Mr. Zooly tried all the harder to keep his animals quiet. He fed his animals all kinds of wonderful food and he fed them lots and lots of it. But the animals were very, very noisy.

Then something happened to make matters worse.

A friend of Mr. Zooly's sent him three big elephants from South Africa.

"Where shall we put them?" said Mr. Zooly. "There just isn't any more room in the zoo."

"We will have to find room for the new elephants," said Mrs. Zooly. "It would be very rude to send them back. Perhaps we could squeeze the lions into a smaller cage and let the new elephants move into the old lion cage."

Now this meant moving the polar bears out of their cages to make room for the lions. This meant moving the monkeys out of their cages to make room for the polar bears. In fact, this meant moving every animal in the zoo to make room for another.

The animals didn't like the idea of moving into smaller cages. So, when Mr. Zooly moved them, they made more noise than ever before.

"Grrr! Eeeeek, Eeeeek! Bark, Bark! Galump, Galump!" said the animals as they moved from one cage to another.

Mr. Crabshaw almost went crazy.

He ran out of his great big house into the street. "Come at once," he said to a policeman standing on a street corner. "Mr. Zooly's animals are making so much noise that I can't eat or sleep or even hear myself think. I insist that you send them all away."

The policeman blew his whistle. Soon a great many policemen and the Chief of Police and Mr. Crabshaw were standing on the porch of Mr. Zooly's zoo. The Chief of Police rang the doorbell.

The lions were roaring. The monkeys were screaming. The bears were growling. The noise was terrible.

When Mr. Zooly came to the door, the Chief of Police said, "You must stop this noise at once. Your animals are disturbing the peace."

"Oh dear," said Mr. Zooly. "I certainly do not

want to disturb the peace and I want my animals to be happy. But I don't know what to do."

And he told the Chief of Police about the new elephants.

"Well," said the Chief of Police, "I'm very fond of elephants, myself, but you must get your animals quiet. I'll give you until tomorrow morning. If you cannot do it by then, the animals must be sent away."

All night long Mr. Zooly worried about his animals. Then early the next morning he had an idea. He went to call on Mr. Crabshaw.

"Mr. Crabshaw," said Mr. Zooly, "why do you live next door to my zoo if the noise bothers you so?"

"I would rather live anywhere else in the world," said Mr. Crabshaw, "but no one will buy my house. It's much too big."

"I will buy your house," said Mr. Zooly. "It will not be too big for my elephants. It will make the best elephant house in the world."

Mr. Zooly bought the house from Mr. Crabshaw that very day. And that night Mr. Crabshaw moved to the other side of town.

Mr. Crabshaw's house became a fine elephant house. The elephants were very happy in it. The other animals were happy, too, now that they were moved back to their own cages.

But that isn't the end of the story. Oh, no. Mr. Crabshaw began to miss the animals after a while. So, every now and then, on Sundays and holidays, he visited Mr. Zooly and his animals. Mr. Crabshaw liked especially to visit the elephants because they were living in his old house.

Aren't people funny sometimes?

THE THOUGHTFUL LITTLE TRUCK

by CATHERINE WOOLLEY

Once there was a little truck that carried dirt. This little truck was always thinking. Sometimes he thought about the pretty flowers in the fields. Sometimes he thought about the gasoline he would have for dinner. But mostly he thought about children, because the little dirt truck loved children.

One day when he was thinking, he thought that he was tired of carrying dirt. He wanted to carry something the children would like. He thought and thought about what he could carry. But he couldn't think of anything.

Then one day he saw a milk truck. It looked as white as snow and the little dirt truck thought, "Maybe I could carry milk."

He said to the milk truck, "I should like to carry milk to hungry little boys and girls. Do you think I could carry milk?"

"Oh no!" said the milk truck. "You're a dirt truck. You couldn't carry milk. You're not clean enough."

"If I was painted white, couldn't I?" begged the little truck.

But the milk truck told him no, he couldn't.

Pretty soon the little truck met a big delivery truck.

He thought what fun it would be to carry parcels to children's houses.

He said to the delivery truck, "I should like to carry new clothes and toys to good little boys and girls. Do you think I could?"

"Oh no!" said the delivery truck. "You're a dirt truck. You couldn't carry parcels. You're not big enough."

"If the parcels were piled up high, couldn't I?" begged the little truck.

But the delivery truck told him no, he couldn't.

Then the little truck met a truck that carried fruit and vegetables. Everything looked nice and fresh, and he thought it would be pleasant to carry ripe tomatoes and juicy oranges and delicious bananas and peaches.

He said to the fruit and vegetable truck, "I should love to carry fresh fruit and vegetables that children like to eat. Do you think I could?"

"Oh no!" said the fruit and vegetable truck. "You're a dirt truck. You couldn't carry fruit and vegetables. You're too bumpety."

"If I went ve-e-ry slowly over the bumps, couldn't I?" asked the little truck.

But the fruit and vegetable truck told him no, he couldn't.

"Well," thought the little truck to himself, "I'll think of something I can carry. And while I'm thinking, I'll be just the best dirt truck that ever was."

So the little dirt truck kept on being a dirt truck, and he kept on thinking. And finally he thought of something wonderful.

He said to his driver, "Aren't you tired of this dirt business?"

The driver said yes, he was.

"Let's start a different business," said the little truck.

"What business?" asked the driver.

"A wonderful business I've thought of," he said. "You guess."

"The milk business?" asked the driver.

"No!" The little truck smiled. "Something better!"

"The delivery business?" asked the driver.

99

"Oh no!" cried the little truck. "Something much better!"

"The fruit and vegetable business?" asked the driver.

The little truck laughed and laughed. "Oh no!" he chuckled. "Something much, much better!"

"Well what, for goodness' sake?" said the driver.

"The merry-go-round business!" said the little truck.

"Why, that's a good idea," declared the driver.

So they bought a little merry-go-round that went merrily round and round.

They bought a music box that played little tinkly tunes. They painted the little truck green and put the merry-go-round and the music box on the truck.

And one sunny morning in May, when the sky was blue and the breeze was warm, the little truck started out. And when he got to a good corner he stopped.

Then the little truck stood very still, and the music box played little tinkly tunes, and the merry-go-round went merrily round and round and from every direction the children came running with pennies for rides. And they rode and rode and rode on the merry-go-round!

After that the little truck traveled all over the

country, giving merry-go-round rides to the children.

He was very happy.

"I thought I'd think of something!" thought the little truck to himself.

SURPRISE AROUND THE CORNER

by CORINNA MARSH

"Wake up, Jimmy," called Mommy. "Time to get up!"

Jimmy opened his eyes and looked around. Where was he? This didn't look like his room. Where were all his toys? And what was that big maple tree doing outside his window? That never used to be there. Everything was different. Everything but Mommy. She was the same, of course.

Then Jimmy remembered. He and his Mommy and Daddy were living in a different place now. This was their new house.

Jimmy woke up some more, and then he remembered about yesterday. Yesterday was the day they moved.

Mommy and Daddy had been packing all the things in the old house for days and days. They had put some things in trunks and suitcases and some in boxes and barrels.

Then, yesterday, the moving men came.

They put all the boxes and barrels and trunks and furniture into their big moving van. Then they closed the doors of the van and rumbled away.

Mommy and Daddy and Jimmy took their suitcases and went in a taxi to the station. Then there was a long, long train ride. After a while the train stopped at a big station. They got off and another taxi took them to their new house.

It was almost nighttime when the moving van drove up with their things. The men opened the doors of the van and out came all the boxes and barrels and trunks and packages and furniture. The men carried them all into the new house. Then Mommy made their beds so they could go to sleep.

Now it was morning, and Jimmy was waking up in his own bed with his own Mommy saying "Time to get up." But he was in the new house. No wonder everything looked different!

Jimmy jumped up and put on his clothes. He ran outdoors to see what the new house looked like from the outside.

It was a pretty house, all shiny with fresh white paint. There were trees around the house. A lilac bush near the porch was full of fluffy purple flowers and smelled like Mommy's perfume.

After breakfast Mommy said, "Come on, Jimmy, let's go to the store and buy some of the things we need."

Daddy waved to them from the front door. He was going to stay home and put the furniture where it belonged.

Mommy took two shopping bags and she let Jimmy carry one of them.

They walked down the street past two other houses. There was a little girl playing with a doll on the porch of the first house. She waved hello to Jimmy and he waved hello to her. They were going to be friends.

A tiny brown puppy came rolling down the lawn
of the next house. He barked a little at first, but
Mommy patted him and then Jimmy patted him.
The puppy wagged his tail. *They* were going to
be friends too.

And now Jimmy and his Mommy came to a corner. "What's going to be around the corner?" he
asked.

"A surprise," said Mommy.

"I think it's going to be an organ grinder with
a monkey," said Jimmy.

But it wasn't. It was the Post Office with an
American flag flying out the window, just like the
Post Office where they used to live.

Mommy and Jimmy went inside and Mommy
told the Postmaster their new address. He wrote
it down in a book.

Then Jimmy and Mommy walked on and came
to another corner.

"What's going to be around *this* corner?" asked Jimmy.

"A surprise," answered Mommy.

"I think it's going to be a hundred elephants," said Jimmy.

But it wasn't. It was the super market, looking just exactly like the one where they used to live.

They went into the super market, and Mommy bought a lot of good things to eat. She carried some of them in her shopping bag and she let Jimmy carry some in his shopping bag.

Then there were more stores. Every time they came to a corner, Jimmy asked, "Will there be a surprise around this corner?"

And Mommy said, "There's always a surprise around every corner."

By this time Jimmy was getting very tired. They had walked around so many corners—he wondered how far they would have to walk now to get home. He thought it must be around lots more corners. He was so tired he began to cry.

"There's a great big beautiful surprise around *this* corner," said Mommy cheerily as they came to the end of the block.

"I don't want any more surprises," cried Jimmy. "I want to go home."

And what do you think the surprise was? There, around that very corner, was Jimmy's own shiny-white new house with the sweet-smelling lilac bush by the porch!

And there was Daddy running down the street to meet them and help them carry their shopping bags home!

Jimmy was SO glad, and he thought his new house was the nicest house in the whole world. It was his home, now.

AUNTIE MARIAH

by BELLA KORAL

Auntie Mariah
Jumped into the fire

The fire was too hot
She jumped in the pot

The pot was too black
She jumped in a crack

The crack was too narrow
She jumped in a barrow

The barrow was too low
She jumped in the snow

Adapted from a version of an old American folk verse.

The snow was too thick
She picked up a stick

The stick it was rotten
She jumped in some cotton

The cotton was so white
She stayed there all night

The night was soon over
So she jumped in some clover

The clover was so sweet
She kicked up her feet

Which made her so dizzy
She got in a tizzy

She cried one two three
And jumped up a tree

She jumped up so high
She soon reached the sky

The sky was so high
She couldn't go higher.

Along came a breeze
And away went Mariah.

Pouf! Pouf! Pouf!

COWBOY BILLY FINDS A HORSE

by LEONORE KLEIN

When Bill Burns was 40 inches tall and 3 years and 364 days old, his father said to him:

"Tomorrow, Billy, will be your birthday. Can you think of something you want for a present more than anything else in the whole wide world?"

"Yes," said Billy, "more than anything else in the whole wide world, I want to be a cowboy."

And so—on the day of Billy's fourth birthday, his mother gave him cowboy boots.

His father gave him a pair of chaps.

His sister gave him a cowboy lasso.

And his brother gave him a cowboy hat.

Billy put on the cowboy chaps, the cowboy boots, and the cowboy hat. He swung the lasso around in the air.

"Now," said Billy. "I'm really a cowboy. But if I'm a cowboy, where is my horse?"

"Your horse!" said his sister. "Now, Billy Burns, what in the world will you do with a horse?"

"Ride him," said Billy.

"How in the world will you find a horse?" asked his father.

"Well," said Billy. "I don't know. But I can't be a cowboy without a horse."

The very next day Billy ran to the corner to talk to Jim, the policeman.

"Good morning, Jim," said Billy politely. "I need a horse. I'M a cowboy now."

"Oho," said Jim. "So you're a cowboy. Well, Trusty here is a very fine horse. But don't you think he's a little too high for you?"

"Oh, no," said Billy very bravely. "I'm a cowboy now and I'm sure I can ride him."

So Jim swung Billy up onto Trusty's saddle.

Billy held on tight to the saddle. He looked at the sky. It was far away. He looked at the ground. It was far away too. Oh, gee. Oh, gosh.

"Please put me down," said Billy politely.

Jim swung him down. "I'm sorry," said Jim.

Billy walked away sadly. Trusty just wasn't the horse for him. Too high.

The day after that, Billy got up early and ran downstairs to talk to Max, the milkman.

"Good morning, Max," said Billy politely. "I need a horse. I'm a cowboy now."

"Oho," said Max. "So you're a cowboy. Well, Charlie here is a very fine horse, but I'm afraid that he won't go very well without the milk wagon."

"Oh, I don't mind," said Billy bravely. "I'm a cowboy now and I'm sure I can ride him."

So Max unfastened the wagon and lifted Billy onto Charlie's back.

Billy held tight to Charlie's mane. He felt slippery without a saddle. But the ground wasn't nearly so far away.

"Giddyap," said Billy. "Giddyap, giddyap."

But Charlie stood still.

Max shook his head and helped Billy down. "I'm sorry, Billy."

Billy went inside sadly. Charlie just wasn't the horse for him. Too slow.

The day after that, Billy rode on his bicycle over to Buttercup Farm to talk to James, the farmer.

"Good morning, James," said Billy politely. "I need a horse. I'm a cowboy now."

"Oho," said James. "So you're a cowboy. Well,

Cobley here is a very fine horse. But don't you think he's a little too fat for you?"

"Oh, no," said Billy very bravely. "I'm a cowboy now and I'm sure I can ride him."

James lifted Billy onto Cobley's back. What a back! It seemed as wide as a kitchen table. Billy stretched and stretched his legs. But they just couldn't reach across Cobley's back.

"I think I'll get down," said Billy politely. "It hurts up here on Cobley's back."

James lifted him down.

"I'm sorry," said James.

Billy rode sadly home on his bicycle. Cobley was just not the horse for him. Too fat.

When Billy got home, he took off his chaps, his cowboy boots, and his cowboy hat. He put his lasso away in the drawer.

"I can't be a cowboy," he said sadly, "without a horse. I'll just be a boy."

Then one day when Billy was riding on his bicycle around the block, he stopped at the big toy store.

He looked in the window and blinked his eyes. He looked again and stared in surprise.

For—there was a horse! A fine, black horse with a black mane, with stirrups and reins—a horse that could rock—forward and backward and forward again. And it didn't look high. And it didn't look fat. And it didn't look slow.

All that summer Billy kept thinking and thinking about that toy-store horse. He kept going past it on his bicycle. In the winter he went past it with his sled. And all the time there were his cowboy boots and his hat and his lasso lying in the drawer.

When spring came Billy rode on his bicycle again past the toy store. Yes! The black horse was still there.

The day came when Billy was 43 inches tall and 4 years and 364 days old. His father said to him:

"Tomorrow, Billy, will be your birthday. Can you think of something you want for a present more than anything else in the whole wide world?"

"Yes," said Billy. "More than anything else in

the whole wide world, I want a horse: a special horse—the big black horse in the window of the big toy store."

And, on the day of Billy's fifth birthday, his mother and father, his sister and brother gave him a horse.

It was a fine, black horse, with a black mane, stirrups and reins—a horse that could rock, forward and backward and forward again. And it wasn't too high. And it wasn't too slow. And it wasn't too fat.

Billy put on his boots and his cowboy hat. He swung his lasso and put on his chaps. Then Billy Burns climbed onto his horse.

"Now," he said. "I'm really a cowboy. Because now I have a horse."

A GOOD MAN AND HIS GOOD WIFE

by RUTH KRAUSS

Once there was a good man and his good wife.

They lived in a beautiful cottage. It had white walls and red curtains and lots of little cubbyholes and handyshelves.

The man and his wife were very happy except that he could never find things.

He would look for his shoes, and he could not find his shoes.

He would look for a book, and he could not find the books.

He would go to feed the canary, and he could not find the birdseed.

But this made no difference because he could not find the canary. He could find nothing.

Then the good man would say, "This is ridiculous!" He would walk up and down the room and shake his head and say very loudly, "This is ridiculous indeed!"

But it was not his fault. He could not find anything because his good wife had moved everything.

She would move the parlor table from the middle of the parlor to a corner of the kitchen, and she would move the kitchen table from the middle of the kitchen to under an apple tree in the garden.

She would say, "My dear, I get so tired of the same things in the same place." Then she would stand back and admire her work.

She moved the clock from the wall above the bed in the bedroom to an end of the mantelpiece in the parlor.

She moved her good man's Sunday clothes from the closet in the hall to the closet in the attic.

She moved his favorite chair from its place before the fire to a corner of the bedroom.

She moved everything in the little house. She said, "Yes, yes, I do get so tired of the same things in the same place!" and smoothed her apron contentedly.

Then the good man had to learn things all over again.

But by the time he learned to find his fishing rod in the broom closet next to the pantry, and his tobacco box in the cubbyhole under the stairs, everything was changed again. Then he looked very stern and cried, "This is ridiculous!" again.

He decided to do something about it. He said, "I will do something about it," and smiled to himself. He said, "I'll settle this once and for all."

And he did something about it.

He put his shoe on his head.

He wore his garters around his neck.

He tied his necktie around his knee.

He wore his trousers for his coat and his coat for his trousers and both of them inside out.

He wore his spectacles on his elbow.

He wore his socks on his ears.

Then he crawled downstairs.

He sat on the breakfast table, ate his napkin and wiped his face on a biscuit.

When the good wife saw him, she opened her eyes wide.

She dropped the dishes. She opened her mouth wide in surprise. She threw up her hands. She cried, "My dear, this is ridiculous!"

He did not reply, but went on buttering his napkin and chewing little pieces off it, and wiping his

face with the biscuit. His garters jingled around his neck and his socks flopped on his ears.

And when she cried again, "But truly this is ridiculous, this is just too ridiculous!" he said very quietly, "My dear, I get so tired of the same things in the same place."

And that was how the good man cured his good woman of a bad habit.

And they lived even more happily than before in their beautiful cottage with its white walls and red curtains and funny little cubbyholes and handy-shelves. And nowadays when he wants to read a book, he knows that he will find it in the bookcase.

FOUND, THE LITTLE LOST DOG

by VAL TEAL

Mother took John and Peter downtown to buy new shoes. They parked their car and got out. A little gray dog was sitting on the sidewalk. He sniffed at John and Peter and whined. They patted his head. He jumped up and tried to lick their faces.

"He likes us," Peter said. "Can't we keep him for our dog?"

"No," Mother said. "He's lost. The people who lost him will be looking for him."

When they came back from buying the shoes, the little gray dog was still there. They patted his head.

"Poor little lost dog," they said.

The little lost dog wagged his tail.

"Can't we keep him for our dog?" John said.

"No," Mother said. "He isn't our dog."

Mother opened the car door. John got in. Peter got in. Mother got in. And then, when nobody was looking, the little lost dog got in. He snuggled down on the floor in the back seat.

When they got home Mother got out of the car. John got out. Peter got out. He left the car door open. The little lost dog got out.

"Look!" Peter said. "It's the little lost dog! He followed us home."

The little gray dog shivered.

"Can't he come in and get warm?" John asked.

"Yes," Mother said. "Poor little lost dog."

They found an old rug and put it in the back hall. The little lost dog lay down on it. They found an old blanket and covered him up. The little lost dog went to sleep.

"We found a little lost dog," Peter said.

"He needs a bath," Father said.

They gave the little gray dog a bath. They washed him with soap. They rubbed him with a

121

towel. He stood on the floor and shook himself.

He wasn't a little gray dog! He was a little white dog! With pink linings in his ears. And a little black nose with pink edges. And a long pink tongue. And beautiful big brown eyes.

They fed him and gave him a saucer of milk.

"Can't we keep him?" Peter asked.

"He isn't our dog," Father said. "We must try to find his owners."

They looked in the evening paper. Nobody had advertised for a little lost white dog.

"Can we keep him now?" John asked.

"No," Father said. "We must try to find his owners."

They took him to a place where all the lost dogs are. They left him there to see if his owners would come and get him. They left him there three days.

After three days they went back. There was the little lost dog. Nobody had come to get him. He was sitting in the corner of a pen. He looked very lost. He looked very sad.

When he saw them he jumped up and ran to meet them. He licked their hands.

"Poor little lost dog," Peter said.

"He isn't lost any more," Father said.

"Can we keep him?" John and Peter shouted.

"Yes," Father said. "Now he is our dog."

They took the little lost dog home. He snuggled down on the rug in the back hall. They covered him up with the blanket. He went to sleep. He looked very happy. He didn't look lost.

"Look," Peter said. "He's found."

So they named the little lost dog Found. And to this very day Found is living with John and Peter and sleeping on the rug in the back hall.

WHY THE LITTLE ELEPHANT
GOT SPANKED

by DOROTHY KUNHARDT

A little elephant was starting out through the forest in his father's big footsteps. "Come back soon," called his mother.

At last the little elephant saw his father. His big father was kneeling down and digging roots with his long tusks.

"Father, when will my teeth be big enough to dig with?" asked the little elephant.

"Quiet, please," said his father.

After the father elephant had eaten his roots, he rested his heavy tusks in the crotch of a tree.

"Does your neck ache, Father?" asked the little elephant. "When it has stopped aching, will you pull up a tree with your trunk?"

"Quiet, please," said his father.

Now the father elephant wrapped his trunk around a big tree. He gave one mighty pull and up came the whole tree out of the ground.

"Father!" said the little elephant. "You're so strong!"

His father looked pleased. He knew he was strong. He knew he was strong as an elephant.

All of a sudden the baby elephant felt like playing. He ran forward and grabbed a branch of the tree with his trunk.

"Ee-eee-eeeee," he squealed. It was a thorn tree! A thorn had pricked his trunk. How it hurt!

He tried to hurry back to his mother, but by mistake he put his two front feet into one deep footprint of his father's and it made him fall. His father came and stood beside him. Very gently he used his big trunk to help the baby elephant up.

Meanwhile the baby elephant's mother was beginning to worry. She was lifting her trunk high in the air to sniff with it and try to smell where her baby was. She was thinking, "When my naughty child comes back, I will show him something else I can do with my long, strong nose!"

When the little elephant came back to his mother, she spanked him. She did not spank him hard.

She was so glad to see him that she really just patted him.

The mother elephant picked a tiny bush with her trunk and put it on her baby's head to keep off the sun.

"Go right to sleep now," she said, "like a good elephant."

The baby leaned up against his mother's tall leg and was asleep in one minute.

EARTH WORM

by MARY MCBURNEY GREEN

I'm an earth worm
Pinky-brown.
When it's dry
I burrow down
Into the cool, cool ground—
I wriggle and I squirm
For I'm an earth worm.

I'm an earth worm
Pinky-brown.
I come up
When rain comes down.
I crawl around
On the cool, wet ground—
I wriggle and I squirm
For I'm an earth worm.

I thicken
And I thin—
When I pull myself in
I wriggle and I squirm
For I'm an earth worm.

LITTLE DUCKLING TRIES HIS VOICE

by MARJORIE LA FLEUR

Once upon a time fat Little Duckling went on a journey into the Wide World. He wandered along the Barnyard Road, and presently he saw the Kitty Cat.

"Me-ow!" said the Kitty Cat.

"O-o-oh!" cried Little Duckling. "Isn't that a pretty sound! I think I'll talk that way!"

But do you suppose Little Duckling could say "Me-ow"?

No indeed!

He tried, but the best he could do was: "Me-e-ack! Me-e-ack!"

And that wasn't pretty at all!

So Little Duckling waddled on and on. After a while he saw Puppy Dog.

"Bow-wow," said Puppy Dog.

"O-o-oh!" cried Little Duckling. "Isn't that a lovely noise! I think I'll talk that way!"

But do you suppose Little Duckling could say "Bow-wow"?

No indeed!

He tried, but this is the way he sounded: "B-ack! B-ack!" And that wasn't lovely at all!

Then Little Duckling waddled on and on. Soon he saw a Yellow Bird in a tree.

"Tweet-tweet-tweet-tweet tweet!" said Yellow Bird.

"Oh, oh, oh!" sighed Little Duckling. "Isn't that a sweet song! I think I'll sing that way!"

But do you suppose Little Duckling could sing "Tweet-Tweet"?

No indeed! He tried his very best, but all he could say was: "Twack! Twack!"

And that wasn't sweet at all!

So Little Duckling waddled on and on. After a while he met Big Cow.

"Moo-o-o!" said Big Cow.

"O-o-oh!" thought Little Duckling. "Isn't that a beautiful roar! I think I'll roar that way!"

But do you suppose Little Duckling could say "Moo-o-o"?

He tried, but all he could manage to say was: "M-ack! M-ack!"

And that wasn't beautiful at all!

Little Duckling was very sad. He could not say "Me-ow" like Kitty Cat. He could not say "Bow-wow" like Puppy Dog. He could not say "Tweet-tweet" like Yellow Bird. He could not say "Moo-o-o" like Big Cow.

He waddled slowly on and on. All at once he saw his own Mother Duck coming toward him along the Barnyard Road.

"Quack! Quack!" cried Mother Duck.

"O-o-oh!" whispered happy Little Duckling to himself. "That is the prettiest sound in the whole Wide World! I think I'll talk that way!"

And he found he could say "Quack! Quack!" very nicely.

PUDDLEJUMPER

by DOROTHEA J. SNOW

Puddlejumper was a little trolley car. He was a good little trolley car even if he was old and his paint was cracked and his wheels squeaked.

Once the little trolley car had been bright and red and shiny and new. Oh, the fun he had had then, clattering and clanging and screeching up and down the streets of the city of Pineville.

"Take it easy, Puddlejumper. Take it easy," Mr. Mopsey, his conductor, would say, putting on his brake a little.

And Puddlejumper would take it easy, for he was very, very fond of Mr. Mopsey. And Mr. Mopsey was very, very fond of him.

For many years Puddlejumper and Mr. Mopsey had taken the men of the city of Pineville to and from work. They had taken the women of Pine-

131

ville downtown shopping and had taken them and their bundles home again. And they had taken the boys and girls of Pineville to grade school and to high school.

Inside the little trolley car it had been cool in summer and warm in winter and dry in the rainy season. Mr. Mopsey had packed them in—the laughing, happy, chattering people of Pineville. Puddlejumper had liked that. Yes, he had liked being full to the bumpers with laughing, happy, chattering people.

Each night Mr. Mopsey had tucked him in the carbarn. He had patted his headlight and said, "Happy day." Then he had left.

And each night Puddlejumper had whispered, "Happy day," in reply, but Mr. Mopsey had never heard him.

Happy days they had been, every one.

But Puddlejumper wasn't happy this morning. Yes, he was draped with bright bunting from bumper to bumper, flags flew from his front and back, and a big bouquet of flowers was fastened to his headlight. But still he wasn't happy.

He was waiting for Mr. Mopsey and, while he waited, tears ran down his front windows and splashed upon his tracks.

132

"Oh, stop your SNIFFLING," snorted the big, new bus that stood near by. "So this is your last day on the streets of Pineville, and tomorrow you will probably be sold for junk. Who cares? Stop your sniffling and let me sleep."

"It's easy for you to talk that way," said Puddlejumper. "You're the one taking my place. I don't want to be sold for junk. I'm still a good trolley car, even if my paint is cracked and my wheels squeak and I have a bare spot or two on my roof."

"Sure, sure," snorted the bus. "Everybody knows you're sound enough to last another thirty years. But you're out of date. You make too much racket with your clatter and clang and screech. You're also too slow, and your tracks are a nuisance in the streets. You're out of date, that's all."

Zzzzzzzzzz, and the big bus fell sound asleep again.

"To be sold for junk!" thought Puddlejumper. "Oh, no, no, no! Never to see Mr. Mopsey again! Oh, my, oh, my!"

Mr. Mopsey didn't look sad that morning. He was whistling when he entered the barn. He was humming when he climbed into Puddlejumper. And he was singing right out loud as he pushed this lever and pulled that to see if Puddlejumper was working all right.

"How can he feel so gay?" thought Puddlejumper sadly. "This is our last day together and he seems positively happy." Puddlejumper sighed. "But then he isn't being sold for junk."

Mr. Mopsey sat down.

"Well, Puddlejumper," he said, "we have a few minutes before we must start, and I am going to tell you a little secret. This is my last trip over the streets of Pineville. They wanted me to run that big bus over there, but I said no, truck driving was not in my line. Going into business for myself, that's what I'm going to do."

The door of the carbarn opened then, and a man waved to them to go ahead.

Rattle, rattle, rattle! Clang, clang, clang! Scre-e-e-ech! Puddlejumper and Mr. Mopsey went out of the carbarn for their last trip over the streets of the city of Pineville.

As they went up and down the streets people lined the sidewalks to watch them go by. "Good-by, Puddlejumper!" they called.

Puddlejumper tried to be gay. Rattle, rattle, rattle! Clang, clang, clang! Scre-e-e-ech! But his heart wasn't in it.

134

Puddlejumper and Mr. Mopsey reached the end of the line. They stopped for a few minutes, as they always had.

Before them was a busy highway. Trucks and busses and cars whizzed back and forth. "Just the place," said Mr. Mopsey. "Just the place."

And he walked to the other end of Puddlejumper and started back.

By the time Puddlejumper and Mr. Mopsey had reached the carbarn, the little trolley car was a sad little trolley car indeed. But Mr. Mopsey wasn't sad. He wasn't sad at all. He stopped Puddlejumper, patted his headlight, said, "Happy day, Puddlejumper," and left, whistling. Happy day, indeed!

For a week Puddlejumper sat in the carbarn. Every day he grew sadder and sadder.

He shivered at the sound of footsteps. When, oh, when was he going to be sold for junk?

Then one day he heard a voice say, "This is the one, Pete." Some strange men put pieces of track up to the back of a big trailer. They rolled Puddlejumper up on it and took him away.

"This is the end," thought Puddlejumper miserably. "This is it."

Then the trailer stopped. The men started to roll him down. Puddlejumper looked around.

"This doesn't look like a junk yard," he thought in surprise. "Why, I know where I am. I am at the end of the line."

Then suddenly he saw Mr. Mopsey. "Let her down here, boys," Mr. Mopsey cried. "Easy now."

And they set Puddlejumper down into a bed of cement.

Then Mr. Mopsey went to work. He cleaned Puddlejumper. He cleaned him thoroughly. He painted his roof with red and white stripes. He put red-and-white striped awnings over his windows. He painted his sides dark green with a tiny bit of yellow for trim.

Mr. Mopsey took out Puddlejumper's seats. He put in a narrow counter and eight stools. In one end he put a tiny kitchen.

Soon the delicious smells of hamburgers, dough-nuts, and coffee wafted out into the busy highway. Trucks stopped, cars stopped, busses stopped. People got out of them. They came up to Puddlejumper and looked at the sign

"TROLLEY CAR INN"

just above his headlight.

"Hmmmm," they said. "How clever." And they went inside.

Puddlejumper is happy now. He is filled all day and far into the night with happy, laughing, chattering people. He is cool in summer, warm in winter, and dry in the rainy season. And Mr. Mopsey is with him, frying, turning, pouring.

Mr. Mopsey pats Puddlejumper's headlight every night as he leaves and says, "Happy day."

"Happy day," Puddlejumper whispers back.

In the distance the lights of the city of Pineville wink at Puddlejumper as he goes happily to sleep beneath the stars.

137

LUKE AND HIS LITTLE
RED WAGON

by RUTH CORDING

Luke was four years old. He had a little red wagon. It was new and bright and very shiny. Luke liked his wagon very much.

Sometimes Luke put rocks in his wagon to make a driveway. Sometimes he put his toys in his wagon and moved them from one place to another. Sometimes he sat in his little red wagon, and Big Brother John pulled it. That was bumpy, but it was lots of fun!

One morning Luke went outdoors to play with his little red wagon. He looked in the garage where Daddy kept his car. But the little red wagon wasn't there!

Then he went to the horse barn where Daddy kept the wagon and harness of his work horses.

But his little red wagon wasn't there!

Luke heard the horses stamping their feet in their stalls.

"Have you seen my little red wagon?" he called out to them in a very loud voice.

But the horses didn't answer. They just kept on stamping their feet and making the hay go "swish-swish."

So Luke went to the cow barn. There were no cows in the barn, for they were out in the pasture. Luke looked all around. But his little red wagon wasn't there!

A little gray kitten was sleeping in the sunshine.

"Have you seen my little red wagon?" Luke asked the gray kitten.

But the kitten didn't answer. She just kept on sleeping.

Then Luke went to the chicken house. There were some hens sitting on their nests. Luke looked all around. But his little red wagon wasn't there!

"Have you seen my little red wagon?" Luke asked the hens.

But the hens didn't answer. They just kept sitting on their nests and saying, "Cluck! Cluck!" to each other.

So Luke went down to the garden. He looked

all around. But his little red wagon wasn't there!

Then he started to walk along between the rows of corn. The corn was very tall. It was taller than Luke. And the leaves went "swish-swish" against his face. He kept looking for his little red wagon. But his little red wagon wasn't there!

Pretty soon wherever Luke looked, all he could see was tall corn. He could not see the garage or the horse barn or the cow barn or the hen house. He felt very hot and very tired and very thirsty. He wished Mother were there, or Big Brother John.

By and by he began to cry a little. Then he cried harder and harder and harder.

After a while he heard his mother calling him.

"Luke! Luke!" she called. "Where are you?"

"I'm right here! In the corn!" he called back to her.

Then he stopped crying. And soon there was Mother coming through the corn after him!

"What are you doing out here in the corn?" she asked.

"I'm looking for my little red wagon," said Luke.

"Oh, Luke!" his mother said, "Come with me! I'll show you where your little red wagon is."

So Luke and Mother walked past the hen house and past the cow barn and past the horse barn and past the garage, and then they came to the shed where Daddy kept his farm tools in the winter.

And there in the middle of the shed—just where Luke had left it—was his little red wagon!

It had some hay in it which Luke had put there. And in the middle of the hay was Mrs. Tabby and five cute little new black kittens!

THE LITTLE DARK HORSE

by VARDINE RUSSELL MOORE

Every afternoon in the park, the red and gold merry-go-round sparkled in the sun. The proud, prancing horses danced round and round while the gay, tinkling music called the children to come take a ride.

There was one little horse very much like the others, but there was something different about him. He was darker than the other horses and he seemed to be listening for something. His ears stood a little straighter. His nose seemed to sniff the air. His eyes almost twinkled.

One moonlight night after all the boys and girls had gone home, the Little Dark Horse felt lonesome. He was tired of going round and round and never getting any place. No matter how fast he went he always came back and stopped at the same spot at the sign: BUY YOUR TICKETS HERE.

He was tired of never moving a little bit to the left or a little bit to the right. He only went up and down and around and around and around.

I wonder where the children go when they leave the park. I wonder what they see. I wonder if I could step down from the merry-go-round and find out, he said to himself.

The Little Dark Horse stepped quietly down from the merry-go-round.

He opened his mouth to see if it would move. AND IT DID!

He blinked his eyes to see if they would blink. AND THEY DID!

He switched his tail to see if it would wag. AND IT DID!

Joyfully the Little Dark Horse started down the highway, gallopy, gallopy, gallopy.

At first, he couldn't help galloping up and down almost as much as he galloped forward. But he soon found that he could go much faster by keeping his feet close to the ground and galloping straight ahead.

After a while, he came to a dusty little country lane. He turned off the highway and galloped along in the dust. It felt so soft and good to his feet.

Soon he stopped galloping. He stepped quietly down the dusty little lane in the moonlight. He lifted his nose and took a deep breath. He could smell honeysuckle growing on a rail fence. It smelled so fresh and sweet.

Now the little horse was getting thirsty. Just then he came to a farmhouse. A well of clear, cool water was in the yard. Beside the well was a bucket, full to the brim. The Little Dark Horse drank and drank until he wasn't thirsty any more. It tasted so cool and good.

By this time, he was tired and sleepy. So he found

a soft spot beneath a big apple tree by the fence, and settled himself comfortably to take a nap.

When I wake up, he said to himself, I'll go and find the children.

When he woke up it was day—a glittering, sunshiny day. He shook himself and stretched himself and started off again. Gallopy, gallopy, gallopy.

Before long he saw a crowd of people going into a place with a high, white fence all around it. A sign on the gate said: COUNTY FAIR. So the Little Dark Horse joined the gay crowd.

Inside, he saw many strange sights. He saw the bearded lady. He saw the thinnest man on earth. He saw a prize bull with a ring in its nose. He saw blue-ribbon pigs and red-ribbon sheep and little lambs that did nothing but cry, "Baaaaaaa!"

He saw a little boy eating pink cotton candy. It looked so good that he reached over the little boy's shoulder and took a big bite. The Little Dark Horse was surprised to find that it melted to sweet nothing in his mouth.

The little boy started to cry, but when he saw how funny the Little Dark Horse looked with pink cotton candy all over his nose, he laughed instead.

The Little Dark Horse heard a trumpet blowing: TOOT-TOOT-TA.

He saw horses galloping around a track. So he ran out and galloped, too. It was fun to go as fast as he wanted to. He passed one horse, then he galloped faster and passed the next horse, and the next, and the next, until he had passed them all.

He galloped so fast that he won the race. The people clapped and clapped, and the children shouted, "Hurray for the Little Dark Horse."

When the shouting was over, the children began to skip away. The Little Dark Horse suddenly felt very lonely standing there by himself.

Then he heard a sound that he had often heard before—the gay, tinkling music of a merry-go-round.

He thought, How good it sounds. So jolly! So

inviting! It's the finest sound in the world. He turned and followed the children, dancing along to the sound of the music.

There it was! Red and gold and sparkling, but not as sparkling as *his* merry-go-round. Children were climbing up on the horses, laughing and calling to each other.

"Look! My horse is spotted!"

"Mine has silver reins!"

"Mine is the biggest horse of all"

The Little Dark Horse jumped on the merry-go-round and ran round and round trying to find an empty space, but there was no room.

He stepped back and stood very still as the horses started moving up and down and round and round. How wonderful it was!

Then he remembered his own merry-go-round. "That is where I belong," he cried.

Without waiting another minute, the Little Dark Horse turned and started back. Gallopy, gallopy, gallopy. He must hurry to get to the park before the children came in the afternoon. So he galloped faster and faster.

He was almost out of breath when he reached the park. There was his own place, still standing empty. The music had not started. He stepped quietly into the empty place.

He was satisfied now, for he knew what the children saw outside the park. He had something to think about when everyone went home at night. He could remember the soft feeling of dust under his feet. He could remember the smell of honeysuckle growing on a rail fence in the moonlight. He knew the taste of clear, cool water.

He had seen glittering sunshine from the shade of an apple tree. He could remember the sound of many voices, cheering and shouting, "Hurray for the Little Dark Horse!"

Although he would never forget his great adventure, he was glad to be back. His eyes almost twinkled. He seemed to be listening for something.

Then he heard the children calling, "I want to ride on the Little Dark Horse."

Now he knew that this was where he belonged, going round and round on a wonderful, sparkling merry-go-round.

LITTLE WIND

by KATE GREENAWAY

Little wind, blow on the hilltop,
Little wind, blow on the plain,
Little wind, blow up the sunshine,
Little wind, blow off the rain.

WHO LIKES THE DARK?

by VIRGINIA HOWELL

The sun goes down loud and bright. But the night comes down soft as a feather dropped from a bird's wing. The day is golden, and the night is silver.

The day is for growing and running and working.

The night is for listening and resting and dreaming.

The dark is like the soft blanket that covers you, but it is blue with silver light. At night the birds nest in trees. Children who play in fields and parks all day rest at night.

For rabbits, lazy woodchucks and skunks, the night is the time to eat.

Then it is safe to get into gardens and garbage cans because people are in houses, asleep.

Night is the cool time.

It brings the dew and the sweet night smells. The dew wets the plants and the grass. The dew is a drink for hot plants and for thirsty animals.

Pine trees smell sharper, roses smell sweeter, and the new-cut grass smells like fresh hay.

The night has light, too—the warm, yellow lights in houses, the strings of lights on the streets.

There are the twinkling lights from the stars and the delicate light from the moon. Shining on the snow, shining on a lake the stars and the moon give a very bright light. And the big dipper keeps time all night long around the North star.

Sailors like the stars to steer their ships by.

Cowboys can ride home horseback, and know their way by the stars.

Night is the time for stories and songs.

Children and mothers and fathers love the special games, the special fun they have just before bedtime.

It is a time for reading, too, and for music and listening.

In bed, in the country, you can hear the near sounds of frogs, croaking in a pond.

You know that they're playing leap-frog and swim-to-the-lily-pad.

From the barn and the pastures are the sounds
you heard in the day, horses neighing, cows moo-
ing, roosters crowing.

Early in the morning and late at night the farmer's truck goes rattling down the road.

In bed in the city there are near sounds.

All day you watched the cars and busses, the
fire-engines and trucks.

Now you hear the honking of horns, the whirr
of motors, the squeaking of brakes, the policeman's
whistle and the clanging of bells.

You hear the sounds, but you remember how
the cars look racing down the street, stopping for
red lights, how the policeman blows his whistle,

and how the firemen ring the bells on the engine.

In bed, in the city and the country, there are the far sounds. They are the sounds that make you dream.

The rain on the window-panes and the whistle of the wind make you feel snug and warm in bed. You sing to the wind or say a rhyme to the patter of the rain. You hear the voices of your mother and father and they make you think of how it will be to grow up.

There are trains you watched in a station, rushing down the tracks, blowing their whistles, far away—away to cities and farms, mountains and beaches you'd like to see.

Later the night grows quiet. Then almost everybody is asleep.

You are asleep.

It is cool.

Before you know it the milkman delivers the milk to your door.

Birds sing and fly.

Cats meow to go out-of-doors.

You hear the sound of cars going up and down the streets. The sun comes up, and lights your room.

And you wake up.

It is day again, the golden day for running and playing, after a good night's rest.

LITTLE

by DOROTHY ALDIS

I am the sister of him
And he is my brother.
He is too little for us
To talk to each other.

So every morning I show him
My doll and my book;
But every morning he still is
Too little to look.

157

THE LITTLE CAT THAT COULD NOT SLEEP

by FRANCES MARGARET FOX

Once there was a little cat who wanted to stay awake all night. So she pretended that she could not sleep.

She was a polite, gentle cat, but she made all her friends uncomfortable because she was so restless.

She used to go walking around, and walking around, waving her tail . . .

One evening when the farmer milked his two cows and the farmer's wife came out of the house with a pail full of milk for the cat family's supper, Little Cat decided that *she would stay awake all night.*

The mother cat and all the kittens lapped and lapped the milk until it was gone. Then they went back to the barn and settled down on the hay and went to sleep, all but Little Cat.

Little Cat was getting sleepy, too, but she would not lie down. She rubbed her eyes and said, "I shall stay awake all night!"

So Little Cat walked out of the barn and up the hill to the house.

She watched the big dog lie down on the porch, put his head on his paws, close his eyes and go to sleep. But Little Cat thought, Not I! I shall stay awake all night!

Little Cat ran down the hill again and tried not to count the sheep as they walked through the farmyard gate to their shelter for the night. They all settled down and went to sleep.

"But not I," said Little Cat, "I shall stay awake all night!"

She watched the horses, and the cows, and the pigs go to sleep, but although she felt sleepier and sleepier herself, Little Cat said, "Not I. I shall stay awake all night."

But it is not much fun to stay awake all night unless you have company. By this time all the animals on the farm were sound asleep and there was no one for Little Cat to talk to.

She decided to go to the zoo and visit some of the animals there. Surely there would be some other animal from around the wide world who liked to stay awake all night.

On the way she saw a robin in a tree. The robin was asleep with his head under his wing. She saw two rabbits sleeping rabbit-fashion in the grass, and a squirrel sleeping in a hollow post of the roadside fence.

Pretty soon Little Cat came to the zoo. The first animal that she saw was the African wildcat.

It was a beautiful animal and looked like Little
Cat's mother. At first they gazed at each other.
Then the wildcat yawned and closed its eyes. It
tucked its head close to its body, and began breathing up, down, up, down, and then it was fast
asleep.

Little Cat blinked her eyes wider open and
walked away fast.

Near by in their cages, the porcupines were lying, stretched out, asleep with their noses pointing into the corners.

Little Cat walked away quickly. The raccoons
in their cages were fast asleep in queer positons.

"Well! Well! that's strange," said Little Cat.

And she walked on.

Next Little Cat watched the opossums settle
down for the night. They, too, slept in all sorts
of positions.

One opossum curled into a ball and put his head under his hind leg.

Little Cat could hardly keep her eyes open when she saw those opossums sleeping—sleeping—

She ran all the way to the skunks' cage to keep herself awake.

All of the skunks were sleeping soundly, flattened out like fur rugs.

Little Cat shook herself and walked on as fast as she could.

Little Cat watched the tigers. They yawned terribly before they curled up and went to sleep with their heads toward their hips. Then they began breathing up, breathing down, breathing up and breathing down.

And still Little Cat was wide awake.

Little Cat visited the deer, but they were already sound asleep. Some were lying with their legs folded under them. Some were dreaming with their heads straight out. Others slept with necks curled back and their heads toward their hips, all

sleeping

sleeping

sleeping . . .

Isn't anyone in this whole zoo staying up tonight? Little Cat wondered. But no one was. The hippo-

potamus was lying flat on its stomach with its head straight out in front, resting on the ground, fast asleep.

The monkeys were curled up, or stretched out, or lying on their stomachs or on their backs.

Their eyes were all shut tight and they all were asleep.

The camels were lying down with their four legs folded under them, sound asleep.

"Umpph!" said Little Cat, and walked away, waving her tail.

Stepping high, and still wide awake, Little Cat

163

went to see the elephants. By this time it was after sunset and beginning to grow dark. Three young elephants were lying down.

Other elephants stood with their trunks lying on the ground and they, too, were sound asleep.

They stood first on one foot, then on another foot, on one foot then on another . . . moving and swaying, and snoring.

Little Cat enjoyed watching them.

This is something like it, thought Little Cat. This is really fun. She tucked her legs under her body and cuddled down, so she could watch the show in comfort.

By this time Little Cat had forgotten that she intended to stay awake all night, because she was having such a good time.

With her bright eyes wide open, she watched the elephants swaying and moving, standing first on one foot, then on another; one foot, another foot, one foot, another foot.

One huge old elephant, with his trunk lying on the ground, began to snore louder than all the others put together.

He rocked from side to side, and from head to tail, from head to tail, while all the elephants were moving, swaying, snoring, rocking, one foot, another foot, one foot, another foot, rocking, rocking, rocking, heads, tails, heads, tails . . .

Next thing Little Cat knew she was purring and purring, and nodding her head to keep time with the elephants, swaying, rocking, snoring, one foot, heads, tails, heads, tails, while the twilight faded into darkness and the stars came out one by one—

And in another half second, Little Cat was sound asleep!

I THANK YOU, GOD

by ILO ORLEANS

I thank you, God,
For a hundred things:
For the flower that blooms,
For the bird that sings,
For the sun that shines,
And the rain that drops,
For ice cream,
   and raisins,
      and lollipops. Amen.

166